MW00981358

A LUCKY STAR

Anthea tried to stay calm as she dressed, but then, totally unable to contain herself, as soon as she entered the Saloon, she blurted out to Linette that she had heard from the Earl.

"Papa telegraphed *you* and not *me*?" she pouted.

"I am certain he meant the telegram for both of us," she replied hastily.

"That will be it," nodded Linette, satisfied that she was right.

"I look forward to becoming better acquainted with your father," volunteered Anthea, as casually as she could. "He seems such an interesting gentleman, even if he is a bit of a mystery."

"What makes you say that?"

"I mean the fact that he has never remarried. When did you say your mother died?"

"Oh, I was only two. Mama miscarried and it was later that she succumbed to an internal infection. Papa does not like to talk about it."

"That is so tragic, it must have been awful for him," persisted Anthea. "Eighteen years is a long time for him to be on his own. Have there *never* been ladies in his life?"

THE BARBARA CARTLAND PINK COLLECTION

Titles in this series

A LUCKY STAR

BARBARA CARTLAND

Barbaracartland.com Ltd

THE BARBARA CARTLAND PINK COLLECTION

Barbara Cartland was the most prolific bestselling author in the history of the world. She was frequently in the Guinness Book of Records for writing more books in a year than any other living author. In fact her most amazing literary feat was when her publishers asked for more Barbara Cartland romances, she doubled her output from 10 books a year to over 20 books a year, when she was 77.

She went on writing continuously at this rate for 20 years and wrote her last book at the age of 97, thus completing 400 books between the ages of 77 and 97.

Her publishers finally could not keep up with this phenomenal output, so at her death she left 160 unpublished manuscripts, something again that no other author has ever achieved.

Now the exciting news is that these 160 original unpublished Barbara Cartland books are already being published and by Barbaracartland.com exclusively on the internet, as the international web is the best possible way of reaching so many Barbara Cartland readers around the world.

The 160 books are published monthly and will be numbered in sequence.

The series is called the Pink Collection as a tribute to Barbara Cartland whose favourite colour was pink and it became very much her trademark over the years.

The Barbara Cartland Pink Collection is published only on the internet. Log on to www.barbaracartland.com to find out how you can purchase the books monthly as they are published, and take out a subscription that will ensure that all subsequent editions are delivered to you by mail order to your home.

NEW

Barbaracartland.com is proud to announce the publication of ten new Audio Books for the first time as CDs. They are favourite Barbara Cartland stories read by well-known actors and actresses and each story extends to 4 or 5 CDs. The Audio Books are as follows:

The Patient Bridegroom	The Passion and the Flower
A Challenge of Hearts	Little White Doves of Love
A Train to Love	The Prince and the Pekinese
The Unbroken Dream	A King in Love
The Cruel Count	A Sign of Love

More Audio Books will be published in the future and the above titles can be purchased by logging on to the website www.barbaracartland.com or please write to the address below.

If you do not have access to a computer, you can write for information about the Barbara Cartland Pink Collection and the Barbara Cartland Audio Books to the following address:

Barbara Cartland.com Ltd., Camfield Place, Hatfield, Hertfordshire AL9 6JE, United Kingdom.

Telephone: +44 (0)1707 642629
Fax: +44 (0)1707 663041

THE LATE DAME BARBARA CARTLAND

Barbara Cartland who sadly died in May 2000 at the age of nearly 99 was the world's most famous romantic novelist who wrote 723 books in her lifetime with worldwide sales of over 1 billion copies and her books were translated into 36 different languages.

As well as romantic novels, she wrote historical biographies, 6 autobiographies, theatrical plays, books of advice on life, love, vitamins and cookery. She also found time to be a political speaker and television and radio personality.

She wrote her first book at the age of 21 and this was called *Jigsaw*. It became an immediate bestseller and sold 100,000 copies in hardback and was translated into 6 different languages. She wrote continuously throughout her life, writing bestsellers for an astonishing 76 years. Her books have always been immensely popular in the United States, where in 1976 her current books were at numbers 1 & 2 in the B. Dalton bestsellers list, a feat never achieved before or since by any author.

Barbara Cartland became a legend in her own lifetime and will be best remembered for her wonderful romantic novels, so loved by her millions of readers throughout the world.

Her books will always be treasured for their moral message, her pure and innocent heroines, her good looking and dashing heroes and above all her belief that the power of love is more important than anything else in everyone's life.

"I believe in fate rather than luck and so many women over the years have said to me 'I am down on my luck' or 'fate has been so cruel to me'. I have always replied 'there is so much we can all do to make our own fate work for us – all you have to do is to be really positive and determined about yourself and your life and you will find that mysteriously so much of what you want will unexpectedly come to you'."

Barbara Cartland

PROLOGUE
1878

"What are ye doin' here? Ye're no welcome in this hoos!"

Alistair McGregor peered through the front door of his croft at the finely dressed young man who stood on the threshold before him.

From inside the croft, Lord Hayworth, heir to a vast fortune in the South of England, could hear terrible moans from a woman wracked with pain.

"Please, Mr. McGregor – I saw the midwife arrive an hour earlier. Maureen has been brought to bed, has she not?"

"Aye, and a sorry state it be as well. What with her bein' unmarried and the poor wee one she's about to give birth to will be a boy – "

"Please, don't say the word," cried Lord Hayworth, holding up his hand in dismay. "I know full well what I have done and that is why I am here this evening – to see if there is anything I can do."

"Ye can divorce yer wife and marry our Maureen!" spat out Alistair, his fierce black eyes burning beneath two bushy eyebrows. "And if ye're nay be here to tell her that you'll be makin' an honest woman of her, then ye're not at all welcome."

Alistair McGregor went to close the door, but Lord Hayworth placed his foot between it and the doorpost so it would not shut.

"Please, I beg you! Believe me – I care deeply for Maureen, but a divorce is completely out of the question. My father would disinherit me and then we would all be considerably worse off."

"How can that be?" sneered Alistair, trying to force the door closed.

"I want to help. Let me come inside."

Lord Hayworth held up a small leather pouch.

Instantly Alistair could tell that it contained money.

"I have brought this – " he offered, shaking the bag of coins under the angry man's nose.

He stared menacingly at Lord Hayworth for a full minute before sighing and opening the door to let him in.

"Very well, but if my daughter says she does nae want to see ye, then ye shall kindly leave – but first, I shall have *that*!"

Alistair snatched the pouch as it dangled from Lord Hayworth's elegantly begloved hand and stuffed it inside his jacket before the Lord could change his mind.

Lord Hayworth was not a fool – he knew just how desperately poor the McGregor family was after that year's disastrous harvest, and that the money he had just given to them was more than enough to make sure that they all had food in their bellies through the long winter months.

Lord Hayworth stepped inside the croft.

It was small but homely. There was just one main room with a range and fire burning brightly. On the range, a huge pan of water was simmering.

There was no sign of the midwife, but the dreadful moans from beyond the closed door led him to believe that there lay the room where Maureen was in confinement.

Mrs. McGregor hovered around the stove, throwing

Lord Hayworth filthy looks. She firmly laid the blame for her daughter's plight at his door.

A blood-curdling howl made everyone start.

"I must go to her." Mrs. McGregor wiped her hands on her apron and hurried towards the closed door.

"Please tell her I am here," pleaded Lord Hayworth, who stood ill at ease near the fire.

Mrs. McGregor curled her lip and turned the handle of the door.

Lord Hayworth could see the midwife, hovering at the end of the bed and, for a fleeting second, a tantalising glimpse of a mass of black curls against a white pillow.

"Maureen!" he called out. "I am here."

"Keep yerself quiet if you don't want to be shown the door!" hissed Alistair threateningly.

He was not offered a seat or refreshment. Instead Alistair watched his every move with a sharp eye.

After an hour the midwife emerged from the room to fetch the pan of boiling water.

"Is there any sign of the bairn?" Alistair asked her.

"Nay, none. There are complications – "

"Are ye tellin' me my daughter might die?"

The midwife was firm but unemotional.

"It will be well if ye prepare yerself for the worst," she said, picking up the pan from the stove. "But Maureen is a strong lass – she may yet come through it. Now, will ye open the door for me?"

Alistair opened the door, cast a fearful look into the room and closed it behind her.

Whirling around, he strode over to Lord Hayworth.

"If anythin' does happen to my daughter or the wee bairn, I'll hold ye responsible. Is that clear?"

Lord Hayworth nodded.

He moved away towards the window.

Outside the wind was howling.

In the distance he could see a lantern. Squinting, he tried to make out what or who it was.

"So are ye happy with yerself?" exploded Alistair, who began to pace the room. "A fine wife in the South, but nay, that is nae enough for ye! It was an ill wind that blew ye to Dunsborough – the Lord knows why ye came to haunt me and my kin!"

"I was sent to oversee my father's estates," replied Lord Hayworth, looking away from the window.

He had given up trying to see who was approaching from a distance – it was far too black outside.

"I could not have seen how events would unfold."

"Aye, but ye did not turn a blind eye to my pretty Maureen, did ye? I thought the old days were long gone where the Laird had any maid who took his fancy without havin' to face the consequences. I can see I was wrong!"

He cast another withering look at Lord Hayworth who was, by now, feeling quite ashamed of himself.

What the man said was true – he had not given it a second thought when he had seduced McGregor's beautiful daughter. To him, she had been a pleasant diversion in an otherwise Godforsaken place.

Maureen, with her flowing mass of dark hair, pale green eyes and a ready smile, had charmed him from the first day he had seen her by the brae, leading a goat back to the family's croft.

How delightful he had thought her.

And only a few months later after an amusing and delicious game of cat and mouse, she finally gave herself to him in the heather, clasping him to her soft bosom and sighing in ecstasy.

Lord Hayworth hung his head as he recalled all the words he had not meant that had tumbled so easily from his lips.

He said he did not love his wife and that he longed to escape.

He promised her marriage and then, after she had fulfilled her part of the bargain, he had not.

A tremendous cry erupted from behind the closed door, followed by the yelping of a newborn child.

He waited for the door to open.

At last an exhausted Mrs. McGregor emerged.

"It's a bonny girl," she said wearily, "and Maureen will recover. We almost lost her, but the girl has strength."

"Thank the Lord!" cried out Alistair, lifting his eyes upwards. "And now, me and ye have some serious matters to discuss. Dinnae think that ye can buy us all off with one heavy purse!"

"I have already told you – it is impossible. I cannot marry your daughter."

"And I say, ye will, if I have to put my gun to yer head and see to it meself!"

Insistent knocking at the door interrupted his flow. When there was no answer, the knocking came again even harder and louder.

"Are you going to answer?" asked Lord Hayworth, grateful of the interruption.

Alistair grunted and then went to the door. Pulling it ajar, he was stunned to see a young boy standing there.

"What's yer business?" he demanded sharply.

Outside the wind was screeching and he could only just about make out the boy's face thanks to the lantern that he carried above his head.

"Is my – Lord Hayworth – inside?"

"And ye are?"

"His younger brother."

Alistair pulled open the door and let the boy in.

"Elliot!" cried Lord Hayworth. "What the devil are you doing here? I thought I had told you stay at the Hall?"

"One of the servants told me what was going on," he answered grimly. "They do not treat me like a child –"

"This is none of your concern. Now go back to the Hall and wait for me."

He pulled himself up to his full height and looked his brother in the eye.

"I know what is happening and I am here to rescue the *honour* of our family and McGregor's daughter."

Lord Hayworth's elegant features then broke into a patronising grin.

"What nonsense is this, boy? *You* – come to my rescue? How, pray, do you think you might do that?"

"Mr. McGregor," said Elliot firmly, "my family has wronged yours and so I am here to ask your permission to marry your daughter."

Alistair burst out laughing and threw his head back.

"Why wee laddy! You canna be more than fifteen! But I'll say this for ye – ye are more of a man than this ne'er-do-well, here – boy or no!"

"Elliot, go home now and stop being so ridiculous," sneered Lord Hayworth.

"At least the wee boy has a shred of decency in his body!" shouted Alistair furiously. "Now, are you goin' to divorce that wife of yours and make a honest woman of my daughter – or am I going to have to kill ye?"

From the look on his face, Lord Hayworth realised that these were not idle words. He hung his head miserably and examined the fine stitching on his gloves.

"Well?" demanded Alistair.

"It is impossible – I cannot."

"Then, ye know the consequences!"

McGregor strode over to his rifle that hung on the wall and took it down. Slipping off the catch, he pointed it straight into Lord Hayworth's face.

"Then, ye leave me no choice – " he hissed.

"Stop!" shouted Elliot, throwing himself in front of his brother, pushing the muzzle of the gun away. "I will marry Maureen! I am almost sixteen! But for pity's sake, spare my brother!"

Alistair eyed the boy and slowly lowered the rifle.

"Ye're a fine wee laddy, and I do admire yer spirit. Hayworth, I will let ye go on condition the boy marries my Maureen as soon as she is recovered. Will ye shake on it?"

Lord Hayworth went as white as a sheet.

For all his fine manners and airs, he was a coward. He could not speak, but simply held out his leather-gloved hand to McGregor.

Taking it, he shook it and then turned his back on both Elliot and his brother.

"Ye'd better come in and meet her," he said to the boy in a matter-of-fact fashion. "You will wantin' to see the bairn that will become yer ain."

"You have done a noble thing, Elliot," intoned Lord Hayworth, as the boy was led to the bedroom door. "I shall not forget it."

CHAPTER ONE
1892

"No! No!"

A long wail like that of a wounded animal came from the small frame of Anthea Preston as she let the sheet of paper fall to the floor in the fashionable drawing room of her home in Mount Street, Mayfair.

"Darling! What on earth is the matter?"

Lady Preston came hurrying into the room, her eyes staring with fear as her daughter slowly crumpled in a heap by the blue silk-covered sofa.

"Anthea! Speak to me. What is the matter?"

Sobs wracked her slender frame and tears flooded from her blue eyes. She raised her face to her mother and, unable to speak, simply gestured at the letter on the floor.

Picking it up, Lady Preston scanned the lines of the familiar handwriting. She knew at once who it was from, having seen many an envelope addressed in the same hand over the past six months.

Her expression rapidly turned from bewilderment to sorrow as she finished reading the letter.

"Oh, my darling!" she cried, moving over to where Anthea sat sobbing. "I am so very sorry. Jolyon – he has married someone else?"

"Oh, Mama!" sobbed Anthea. "How *could* he do this to me? How could he?"

"He is such a stupid and selfish young man and he has shown his true colours, you have had a narrow escape."

"But, Mama, I love him! I thought I was going to be his wife and now I find some French trollop has stolen him from me!"

"Darling, I blame Jolyon. I can say now that I am not at all sorry to see the last of him. I know how much you cared for him and, because you did, neither your father nor I voiced our concerns. Anthea – he has proved himself not to be a gentleman and you are well rid of him."

"Then why do I feel just as if someone has torn my heart out? Oh, Mama! I cannot bear this."

"It is better to find out what kind of man he is now, rather than after you have married him. You should keep the ring – he does not deserve to have it back."

Anthea looked at the sparkling diamond solitaire on her finger and immediately wrenched it off.

"Here," she cried, handing it to her mother. "Give it to one of the servants or sell it and use the money for the poor. I don't care if I ever see it again!"

At that moment, Sir Edward Preston came into the drawing room and almost dropped his newspaper when he came across the scene that greeted him.

"What the devil? Anthea dearest. What ails you?"

"Sir Jolyon Burnside has jilted her," answered Lady Preston. "He has married another – he has written from his honeymoon."

"The bounder!" murmured Sir Edward, stopping in his tracks. "Could he not at least come and see her?"

"He is in Paris. Apparently he had met this woman in Biarritz and they were married a week ago. His parents threatened to cut him out of the will unless he owned up."

"I should jolly well think so too! Damn fine people – the Burnsides. Shame they have a cad for a son."

"He always was rather spoiled – " murmured Lady Preston, stroking Anthea's fine hair.

They shared the same colours – harebell-blue eyes, golden-brown hair with a peaches-and-cream skin.

In her day Lady Preston had been a great beauty and she had been very proud when Anthea had been voted *debutante* of the year for the Season. Even the Queen had remarked on how charming Anthea was and both she and Sir Edward had had high hopes for a good match.

Sir Jolyon Burnside was a dashing young Baronet who had been endlessly indulged by his parents and now he had run off to Paris with a common actress, whilst back home in England, his fiancée's world was in tatters.

Lady Preston rang for one of the servants to take Anthea to her room. As she was led away by Mrs. Denton, her old Nanny, Lady Preston closed the drawing room door and turned to face her husband.

"She will have to be sent away."

"What, a holiday?" asked Sir Edward.

"Recuperation. We must do our utmost to shield her from the inevitable gossip. Once news spreads of this, we shall be besieged by the usual round of nosy dowagers with nothing better to occupy themselves."

"Well, there's the house at Loch Earn. I know it isn't the season for house parties or shoots, but she will be well cared for. Mrs. McFee will make a good companion."

"Yes. You are right, as always, Edward. The fine Highland air will do her good and soon she will forget all about Jolyon Burnside."

Tucking the engagement ring into the pocket on her skirt, she went into the study to write a letter to ask Mrs. McFee to make Loch View ready for Anthea's arrival.

'Poor, poor dear,' she said to herself, as she dipped her nib into the inkwell. 'Only twenty and so much to look forward to. I could murder Jolyon Burnside! However, he is best forgotten now.

'The sooner she gets to the Highlands, the better. Yes, Scotland will be good for her.'

*

The following week Anthea was put on the train to Scotland. Her parents came to Euston Station to see her off and her maid, Sally, accompanied her as chaperone.

At Edinburgh Station they were met by the family's carriage to take them on the long journey to the village of Loch Earnhead, where their house overlooked the Loch.

Anthea spent six months at Loch View and for the first month did not leave her room. Both her parents came to celebrate Christmas with her that year and then returned home to Mayfair.

Slowly she began to recuperate.

As spring bloomed at Loch Earn, so did she.

"I think I am almost ready to return to London," she told Sally, as they walked by the Loch one day. "I shall write to Mama and tell her that I shall come home for her birthday in June."

"She will be very pleased to see you, miss," replied Sally, who was longing to return to London to see her own family again.

But no sooner had she made plans to travel back home than a dreadful telegram arrived one day in late May.

Mrs. McFee was grey as she accepted the missive that had been brought out by the postman from the village.

'I hope this isn't more bad news.' said Mrs. McFee to herself, as she carried the telegram to where Anthea sat in the garden, enjoying the sunshine. 'That poor lassie has had more than enough with a broken engagement.'

But as soon as Anthea had opened the telegram and read it, Mrs. McFee's worst fears were confirmed.

Trying to keep her composure, Anthea stifled a sob and simply handed it to her so she might read for herself the awful news.

"Her Ladyship! Oh, Lord have mercy!"

Having read it, Mrs. McFee ran inside and straight down the back stairs to the servants' hall.

"Finlay," she cried, as the old butler came hobbling into the room. "Assemble all the servants at once. I want everyone here – everyone! Her Ladyship has died."

*

The funeral was a very grand affair.

Most of Society turned out to pay their last respects at St. George's Church, Hanover Square.

Anthea tried her best to stay composed, but seeing her grieving father was almost too much for her.

"Don't you worry, Papa. I will not leave you," she sniffed, clasping his arm as they walked back.

"Promise me?" he responded, tears glistening in his eyes. "I could not bear it if I lost you as well."

Anthea knew only too well what he meant – he did not wish her to marry and leave the house in Mount Street.

Forcing herself to smile, she squeezed his arm.

"Of course, I promise. I will not leave you."

*

Life at Mount Street soon fell into a routine and the years flew by.

Anthea had stood by her promise to her father and steadfastly spurned the advances of any young man whom she might encounter.

After a while her admirers found themselves others

to marry and visits from potential suitors to Mount Street became less frequent.

Anthea found herself staring out of the window one day at a young couple in the street outside. They were arm in arm and laughing, locked into their own private world.

'They both appear so in love,' reflected Anthea, as they looked into each other's eyes with obvious adoration, 'and now I am so old – *twenty-six* this year – no one will have me. I am destined to be an old maid.'

It was without any hint of regret that she regarded them. She recalled a time when, with Sir Jolyon Burnside, they had strolled gaily through Hyde Park as his carriage followed behind them.

He had bought endless bunches of fresh flowers for her from Covent Garden market.

'And now, no man will ever buy me flowers again – apart from Papa,' she mused, as his carriage drew up.

He often brought her a bouquet to cheer her up as if to make up for potential sweethearts that were long gone.

She heard the front door open and Fricker take her father's hat and coat. She counted down the seconds until he entered the drawing room with a benign smile for her.

"Anthea, dearest," he called out, handing her some flowers. "These are for you."

"Thank you so much, Papa," she murmured, taking the fragrant blooms from him. "Freesias! My favourites."

"Darling, you have been looking a bit pale of late," he remarked, making himself comfortable in the armchair.

"Papa, you must not concern yourself, it is just that I have not been able to shake off this horrible cold. It has been so persistent."

"It has been some time since you last had a holiday, is it not?"

"Well, we went to Brighton for a long weekend last August. Does that not count?"

Her father laughed.

"Anthea, I have been thinking that you have kept me wonderful company since your Mama died without any thought to your own happiness. You are such an excellent daughter and now, I want to show you my appreciation."

"But, Papa," she protested. "You make it sound as if it has been a chore looking after you. I love you dearly and I would not have had it any other way."

"Even so, Anthea, I am aware that you have made certain sacrifices so that you could remain at my side."

He looked at her meaningfully and Anthea blushed. She knew what he was hinting at.

"So, with this in mind, I have decided to send you away on a really long trip. Just you and your maid – or a companion, if you so choose."

"Papa!"

"Every young lady should do the Grand Tour and circumstances have hitherto prevented you from embarking upon such a trip. I am capable of looking after myself for a few months and the Season is in full swing, so I shall not want for entertainment or company. You leave for Paris in a fortnight and return in September."

"Oh, Papa! Thank you," she cried, running over to him and throwing her arms around his neck. "I should like Sally to be with me. She is as good a friend as any I have. So few of my female friends are still unmarried – and I am not certain that their husbands would be too happy to allow them to swan off to the Continent for the summer."

"Well, there is the Dowager Duchess of Markyate. I know she is only a very distant relative, but I am certain she would be happy to accompany you if you would prefer her to travel with you."

"And I should be really bored that I would go out of my mind with her! No, Sally is young and vivacious and she will be the perfect companion."

"Excellent! The arrangements are in place. Now, I must run along, dearest – I have a rather dull dinner at Lord Morton's house tonight and I expect he will want to play cards until the small hours. Do not wait up for me."

With that he rose and kissed her on the cheek.

'Europe!' thought Anthea, dancing round the room and hugging herself. 'Paris! Vienna! Florence! Greece!'

She felt as if, at last, she had been set free from her gilded cage.

'For a few months I will not have to play the dutiful daughter,' she said to herself, as her spirits soared. 'And maybe, I will find a little romance – '

The very thought pleased her enormously as she ran upstairs to tell Sally the wonderful news.

'A trip abroad,' she said to herself joyously. 'I feel as if I have been given a second chance for happiness.'

*

That summer was the best Anthea had ever spent.

Once she stepped off English soil, she felt as if she was a different person. Whilst she still missed her home, the sights and sounds of the greatest Cities of Europe were sufficient to occupy her.

She wandered round the galleries of Paris, admiring fine works of art, and enjoyed the very best *gateaux* in the teahouses of Vienna.

Rome was steeped in so much history and Venice so romantic that by the time they arrived in Crete, she felt as if her life in England was but a distant dream.

She wrote religiously every week to her father and eagerly awaited his replies. As he had planned her itinerary down to the last detail, there was always a cheerful letter waiting for her whenever she arrived at a new destination.

Then one day the letters stopped.

'This is extremely odd,' she mused as they arrived in Athens, 'as Papa always makes certain there is a letter to greet me, maybe the Greek postal service is not as efficient as it is elsewhere.'

But, by the time their stay came to an end, there had still been no word from him.

At last, worried sick, Anthea telegraphed the family Solicitor as soon as they disembarked in Dubrovnik, fearful of what news might be waiting for her in England.

But the reply from Mr. Linton was as shocking as it was unexpected.

She stared and stared again at the telegram, hoping that she would awake and find that it was not true.

"What is it, miss?" enquired Sally.

"We must go home at the end of the week," replied Anthea in a daze. "Papa has married again and is on his honeymoon already. He returns to London on Saturday."

"Lawks!" cried Sally, dropping a pile of washing.

"Hush, Sally, do not curse. We will only be cutting our trip short by a week or two."

"But you so wanted to see Naples, miss. And we were to visit it on our return journey."

"There's no time for Naples now. I shall have the hotel contact the Ticket Office at once and arrange for us to sail back to England instead of going on to Ljubljana."

Sally watched her Mistress closely as she tidied her hair and then left their suite to speak to the Concierge.

"Well! I never. The Master remarried? Whatever next?" muttered Sally.

*

Anthea and Sally arrived back in Mount Street the day before her father and his new wife.

None of the servants would tell her a thing and it appeared as if the new Lady Preston had fallen out of the clouds.

No one knew much about her, save that she was a wealthy widow and about the same age as Sir Edward.

Anthea could not imagine anyone taking the place of her mother and, even before the new Lady Preston had set a foot in Mount Street, had made up her mind that she was not going to like her.

The day of her father's return, Anthea had all the servants, dressed in their best uniforms, turned out in the hall to greet him.

Sir Edward seemed very different when he got out of the carriage, and did not, as Anthea expected, run and sweep her up in his arms and kiss her.

Instead he patted her shoulder as he drew level with her and introduced her to his new wife.

The new Lady Preston was a tall woman with thick black hair and eyes the colour of rainwater.

She stared at Anthea without smiling and flinched slightly when Sir Edward ordered Anthea to kiss her.

Over the next few days Anthea often found herself on the wrong end of her tongue as she criticised everything in the house, including the servants, the furnishings and the way that the sun did not come into the morning room until after luncheon.

But the greatest change was in her father – he was not the loveable man she had left behind in Mount Street. There were times when he was almost a stranger to her.

Then one day as Anthea was wandering around the garden when she overheard her stepmother's strident voice wafting loudly through the French doors.

"Really, she is such a bore," she heard her say. "I confess I cannot stand the sight of her whey face around the place."

"Then you must marry her off and quickly," replied her friend. "We must line up a series of suitable gentlemen who would be willing to marry her. I must admit, Frances, she is not as young as she could be, so we might find it a difficult task."

Anthea then moved a bit closer to the French doors to hear more clearly.

"It's what I intend to do," replied her stepmother. "And I agree – she is a little old to be matched up, but there must be some men from good families who are available. A widower, perhaps?"

"*The dregs* – " answered her friend.

"I would not care if he was the Hunchback of Notre Dame, my dear, as long as he has a good income and can look after her," her stepmother laughed. "The sooner I get her off my hands, the better!"

Anthea staggered back into the garden as the two women inside dissolved into peals of laughter.

'So, this is to be my fate?' she sighed, tears filling her eyes. 'And, as for Papa, I do believe that he will turn a blind eye to her plotting.'

Moving out into the sunshine, she turned her face to the sky and sent a silent prayer up to her mother.

'Who can I turn to Mama?' she implored, 'am I to be treated like a parcel of laundry? *Please*, if you can hear me – help me! For Heaven's sake, help me!'

CHAPTER TWO

Anthea spent the night agonising over ways to stop her stepmother in her tracks.

What her friend had said was true – there were not many, if any, eligible young men about and although she could never imagine her father allowing his new wife to hitch her up to an elderly man, he might in his present state of thrall.

It was not as if the family was in need of the money that a wealthy man might bring, as her father's investments were shrewd and there was plenty to go round.

So on the next day when her stepmother announced that she was going to throw a grand ball next weekend, Anthea knew only too well what lay behind the idea.

"That sounds splendid," said her father. "This house has been silent for too long, in fact, I cannot remember the last time we had music and dancing."

"It will provide an ideal opportunity for me to meet some of your friends and business partners, Edward, and for you to become acquainted with mine."

"Spend as much as you like, Frances, I am feeling in a generous mood as I have just had news that one of my factories has been sold for an extremely large profit."

Lady Preston rose and kissed him on the lips.

Anthea was shocked at this display of affection and although her Mama had loved her Papa dearly, she would never have behaved in such a way in front of the servants!

She caught Anthea's disapproving look and simply smiled to herself.

"And, with that in mind, I have made arrangements for you to visit Monsieur Henri's shop in Bond Street this afternoon," she added, staring at Anthea. "You must be the loveliest girl there and I want everyone to admire you."

"But I don't need a new ball gown!"

"Nonsense. A woman can never have too many. Besides, you do not want to let your father down, do you? Imagine what people will say about him if he does not pay for a new gown for his only daughter."

"Quite," agreed her father. "You are most fortunate that Frances is such a considerate woman, organising a trip to Monsieur Henri's like that."

Anthea sighed inwardly.

The change in her father was extremely unnerving. When her mother was alive, he would have at least listened to her before dismissing her opinion.

"And, by the way, Sally has handed in her notice."

"I beg your pardon?" exclaimed Anthea.

"Yes, Fricker informed me first thing this morning. It appears that her parents have been left a shop in Kentish Town and she is going to work in it with them."

"That is a great pity, I shall miss Sally," stammered Anthea miserably.

She was wondering who she could now have to talk to. The house would be a very lonely place without Sally.

And as for trips away –

The spectre of the Dowager Duchess of Markyate hung over her like a grim shadow.

"Servants are ten a penny," added Lady Preston. "I have asked Fricker to send out to the agency for a new one.

I will do the interviewing myself this afternoon whilst you are out shopping."

"But surely, as you are hiring a new maid for me, I should be here?" ventured Anthea.

"Nonsense, you are far too inexperienced to be able to judge the character of a servant. Besides I am now the Mistress in this house and *I* shall employ the servants."

Anthea wished she could reply that had she married Jolyon Burnside, by now she would have a large house of her own to run with numerous servants.

But she knew that if she started an argument with her stepmother, it would only upset her father.

"Rest assured, Anthea, by the time you return from Monsieur Henri's, I will have engaged someone suitable."

Anthea dreaded to think about the sort of maid she might designate as being 'suitable'.

'If she is so keen to get me off her hands, might she not employ a sour-faced old crone at the end of her useful life? Or worse, a young ambitious maid who will want to snoop and pry into my private affairs.'

Excusing herself she ran to fetch her hat and coat.

'I really need a great deal of fresh air,' she thought, as Fricker opened the front door for her.

Outside the day was overcast and chilly.

'I wish I did not feel so uncomfortable in my own home,' she grumbled to herself. 'I was so looking forward to coming back after my Grand Tour and yet I felt more at home in those hotels than I do now in Mount Street!'

After a bracing walk, she arrived back in good time for luncheon.

Lady Preston had ordered a light meal of soup and rolls as, she said, she did not want Anthea disgracing them by inflating her waistline with a heavy luncheon.

"I don't want Monsieur Henri thinking that I have an overfed heifer for a stepdaughter," she remarked tartly.

Anthea's delicate waist was no more than nineteen inches and, even with the new fashions that called for ever-tighter lacing, she still fitted effortlessly into every design.

By contrast her stepmother's figure was somewhat lumpen and underneath her long sleeves Anthea could see that she was a rather chubby woman.

'Mama was so slender,' she thought, trying not to stare at the roll of flesh popping over the top of her corset. 'What on earth *does* Papa see in her?'

"Fricker will tell us when the carriage is ready. I hope you do not mind going without a chaperone, Anthea, I simply cannot spare you a servant at present. This house is filthy and I have had to make them clean it again."

Anthea opened her mouth to protest, but something told her to hold her tongue.

Although it was true that the house could do with a lick of paint and new wallpaper, the servants always kept it spotless even when there was no one in residence.

She so hoped that her stepmother had not offended Fricker – he was such a valuable and loyal man, that she did not know what they would do if he became disgruntled and decided to seek a post elsewhere.

As they were finishing luncheon, Fricker came in and announced that the carriage was ready.

Anthea rose from the table at once, grateful she did not have to spend any further time with her stepmother.

"Monsieur Henri has been given strict instructions to make you the belle of the ball," mouthed Lady Preston, as Anthea put on her coat in the hall, "he has been told that money is no object and to do his utmost for you."

Although Anthea had gone shopping for gowns on

her own, she had not visited Monsieur Henri's shop before as she had always considered it far too grand.

She climbed into the carriage and sat back to enjoy the short journey to Bond Street and after a few minutes, they drew up outside Monsieur Henri's shop.

Anthea felt quite nervous as she stepped down onto the pavement. Taking a deep breath, she put her hand on the brass door handle of the shop and pushed.

Almost as soon as she set her foot inside, an elegant middle-aged woman in black came towards her.

"Do I have the honour of addressing Miss Anthea Preston?" she intoned in a precise voice.

From her clothing and the way she carried herself, Anthea had expected her to be French and was surprised when the woman was obviously English.

"Why – yes!" stuttered Anthea, quite overtaken by the richness of her surroundings.

"Come with me, please."

The woman led her to a showroom at the rear of the premises. They passed through a wide velvet curtain and the assistant then indicated that Anthea should take a seat in one of the plush velvet chairs.

"Now, allow me to bring you a cup of tea?"

"Thank you."

Anthea took off her gloves and hat and waited.

She had been to many a couturier's establishment and knew what would happen next.

Sure enough, a dimutive man with a moustache and dressed in an immaculate suit appeared in the doorway.

"Mademoiselle Preston? *Enchanté*!"

He rushed over and took her hand, kissing it lightly – then, held her at arm's length while his beady black eyes swept over her form.

"*Très elegante*," he then declared, "*et si belle*. Lady Preston did not say 'ow lovely you are!"

Anthea smiled to herself.

It did not come as any surprise that her stepmother had praised her to Monsieur Henri.

He clapped his hands and out of nowhere appeared two young girls dressed in beautiful ball gowns.

"Elise and Jeanne will model my latest designs," he announced in his flamboyant French accent.

They glided over the carpet towards Anthea so that she could examine the dresses.

One was of oyster silk and the other rose pink.

Both boasted daringly low necklines and, although lovely, Anthea shook her head. She knew that it would be immodest for her to display so much flesh.

Monsieur Henri dismissed the two girls and in their place came another two.

This time Anthea made a close inspection of one of the gowns, a silver creation with puffed sleeves and a more modest neckline.

"Would Mademoiselle care to try it on for 'erself. It is 'er size."

Anthea blushed.

'How does he know what size I am when he has not had me measured yet?' she wondered.

"Madame Morrison will escort you to the changing rooms. I 'ope you do not mind, but another young lady is in there. We are very busy at the moment, but I promised Lady Preston I would squeeze you in."

"Not at all," replied Anthea, her curiosity aroused.

Madame Morrison stepped forward and gestured to Anthea to follow her and as she passed Monsieur Henri, he murmured,

"If Mademoiselle will permit it, I also 'ave a very special gown – *très chic* – that is just your size. I will 'ave it brought over if you would care to see it?"

"Yes, I would love to try it on."

Already she was feeling that she could place herself in Monsieur Henri's hands as she had, so far, been very impressed with his gowns – even if the first ones were not entirely suitable.

Madame Morrison took her to the changing room and sat her down inside one.

"Please wait here. I will leave the curtain open."

On the other side of the room was another cubicle over which the curtain was drawn and she could hear the sound of voices.

Inside a young woman was complaining about the tightness of a sleeve.

"If I am to travel to Italy, I shall bake in this!" she moaned in a girlish voice.

"But your father will not allow you to wear a short sleeve," answered the assistant firmly.

"Papa knows nothing at all about fashion," retorted the girl behind the curtain, "and in any case, he will not be with me for the voyage to Italy."

"No doubt he is very occupied with his business."

"Yes, *boring* ships! I so wish he owned something more interesting – a department store or, perhaps, a stable of fine horses for stud."

Anthea smiled to herself.

Had she not often thought the same thing herself of her own Papa's business?

"I really don't want to travel to Italy," grumbled the girl. "But Papa says I must. Oh, it will be so dull! I am there to make conversation to his boring customers and to look attractive. He says a pretty face helps sell his stupid ships, but I would far rather be in London and have fun."

"But Italy is so beautiful and the people are said to be charming and vivacious," came back the assistant. "We have lots of customers who praise it to the skies."

"It would not be so bad if I had someone my own age to accompany me, but they are always ancient crones with disapproving faces. Papa insists I have a chaperone and now the woman who was to go with me has broken her leg and cannot travel.

"He says he does not have time to find another for me and so he has gone to an agency to find one. I shudder to think what they will root out for me – probably some old horror in a mobcap who will make me wear sailor dresses and pinafores!"

"Yes, it's a shame you cannot find someone a little older than you are but who is still young and lively. Now, please take off the dress and I will ask Monsieur if we can do something with those sleeves."

Anthea heard the girl sigh, then the rustle of fabric as she took it off.

She waited until she heard the swish of the curtain as the assistant left and then she peeped out of hers.

The curtain was half drawn, but there was a gap and she could now see the slim figure of a young girl probably no more than twenty with dark hair and a sulky expression.

She was fiddling with the belt of her dressing gown and looking thoroughly miserable.

Before she knew what she was doing, Anthea was up on her feet and standing outside the other girl's cubicle.

The girl looked up and smiled at her.

"Terribly dull isn't it? I hate buying new clothes."

The girl was very pretty with deep blue eyes and a sweet heart-shaped face, her skin was as white as snow that made an attractive contrast with her dark hair.

"I want to wear grown-up clothes, but Papa insists on making me dress like a child."

Anthea laughed.

"Yes, my Papa can be quite strict with me and I am a good deal older than you."

The girl eyed her carefully.

"But not by much, if I am a good judge."

"I am twenty- six," replied Anthea.

"Oh, that is more than I thought," answered the girl, distractedly. "I am just twenty, but Papa treats me as if I was twelve."

"It's the way with fathers – until the day we marry, of course," added Anthea.

"Ugh! I don't think I could ever marry. I find most men so dull like the men Papa does business with."

"I hope that you don't mind but I could not help but overhear you just now. You are bound for Italy?"

"Yes, Naples. Have you been there?"

"No, not yet. I was in Italy in the summer, but we were forced to curtail our trip and so did not visit Naples as we had planned."

"Oh, that is a pity, I was really hoping that someone might tell me how exciting it was – and then, I would not feel so hard done by."

"Surely it will be an adventure?"

"Not really. I expect I shall be stuck with a lot of old men, making tedious conversation. I don't speak much Italian and my Papa tells me that his customers – he builds ships, by the way – do not speak English. Oh, I know Papa is doing important work and promoting Britain, but I wish it was not so *boring*!"

"Ship building is an important business, we British are famous for our Navy and we are admired by the entire world for our prowess on the ocean."

"That is what Papa says. You must meet him, you and he would get on very well. It sounds as if you would enjoy this trip far more than I would."

The assistant came back with the dress for the girl to try on and another assistant followed her close behind holding the dress for Anthea.

"Do come along, my Lady," the assistant urged her sternly. "Your Papa said that his carriage would return for you at half past two and it is now a quarter past."

The girl smiled apologetically at Anthea.

"I am sorry, I must try this on. Oh, how rude of me – I have not introduced myself, I am Linette Hayworth, my father is the Earl of Hayworth – what is your name?"

"Anthea. Anthea Preston."

Linette thrust her hand through the curtain.

"So nice to meet you, Anthea. Are you rushing off very soon?"

"Well, no –"

"Good, I would love to chat some more with you. I confess I do not always find it easy to speak to strangers – which is why I hate these trips of Papa's so much, but it is as if I have known you for ages."

"Miss Preston?" said the second assistant, thrusting the silvery gown at her.

Anthea's mind was whirling as the assistant helped her into the dress.

'Could it be that Linette has inadvertently given me the solution to my problems?' she thought. 'What if I was to offer to accompany her to Italy? I was so disappointed we did not see Naples and I speak fluent Italian. Surely her father would have no objection to me – a young woman of good family and it would save him the agency fees!'

By now Monsieur Henri was making the finishing adjustments to the gown and Anthea was feeling excited.

She could not wait to talk to Linette again.

"*Parfait!*" he exclaimed. "Mademoiselle will be ze belle of ze ball in zis gown!"

Anthea looked up and gasped.

What Monsieur Henri said was true, even she could see how lovely she now looked in this gown. The silvery material threw lights onto her face and made her skin like pearls, while her eyes seemed bluer than ever.

"Yes," she murmured, "I will take it. Can you have it delivered to my home by Saturday morning? It is most important that I have it for this weekend."

"*Bien sur*, and now, another gown for you."

Just then Linette poked her head around the curtain.

"Anthea," she whispered. "I have just had the most exciting notion. What if you were to come to Italy and be my chaperone? Do you think that would be possible?"

Anthea giggled.

"Linette, you are a mind reader! I was about to suggest the very same thing."

"My carriage has arrived and I must go to another appointment, but are you free later, say in an hour or so?"

"Yes, I am."

"Can you meet me in the restaurant at Fortnum's? We can have tea and discuss this matter further. Say you will – *please*, say you will!"

"I will be there. Half-past three it is!"

Linette hugged herself ecstatically as she left the changing room.

Anthea felt incredibly light – as if she could fly.

The assistant brought a primrose-yellow dress with oyster coloured lace that Anthea thought would be perfect for the Italian climate, so she bought that as well, along with a matching pelisse for the evenings.

By the time she was finished at Monsieur Henri's, it was almost a quarter past three.

Hurrying outside she found her carriage waiting for her and jumped into it.

"Fortnum and Mason's," she ordered, feeling really deliciously wicked for not going straight home.

*

Her heart was beating wildly as she took the tiny lift in Fortnum's. As it stopped at the fourth floor, she got out and looked around for Linette.

"Excuse me, madam, are you, by any chance, Lady Linette's friend?"

A waiter dressed in a black frock coat came up to her almost as soon as she had stepped out of the lift.

"Why, yes."

"Follow me. Her Ladyship is looking out for you."

The waiter led her to a table by the window where Linette was already studying a large trolley of cakes.

"Mmm, shall I have lemon cake or the chocolate?" she pondered, one finger in her mouth like a small child.

Anthea could not help but smile.

Linette was no more than a child after all and very young for her age despite mixing with adults so frequently.

"Chocolate," answered Anthea firmly.

"Say you have thought it over and you *will* come,"

implored Linette, a small frown creasing her lovely young brow. "I have quite set my heart on it!"

She pouted as she spoke and dipped her head shyly.

"I would love to," exclaimed Anthea, as the waiter hovered over their takes.

Linette leaned over and squeezed Anthea's hand.

"I am certain that Papa will be thrilled when I tell him not to bother with the agency."

"When do we leave?"

"Oh, promise me that you will not go back on your word – " Linette hesitated before continuing, "Papa's ship sails next Monday from Portsmouth."

"Goodness me! That soon?" cried Anthea, putting down her teacup. "I had not thought – "

"Please say you will still come," entreated Linette. "I don't think I could bear it if you do not!"

Anthea stirred her tea and thought.

If the ball was on Saturday evening, then, it would mean leaving London on Sunday evening –

"Very well," she said after a lengthy silence. "But are we to travel down to Portsmouth together?"

"Of course. Papa will let us use his fastest horses and his best carriage. We shall meet him in Portsmouth, as he will already be there with his ship."

"There is something crucial I must confide in you, however," added Anthea quietly. "It would be very unfair to keep you in the dark – I shall be running away."

"Goodness! From your family?"

"I will tell you the story on the trip, but briefly Papa has remarried and my stepmother has made it clear that she wishes to be rid of me. However, her plan is to marry me off to the first man who offers for me. The reason I was at

Monsieur Henri's today was to buy a new gown for a ball at the weekend. The express purpose of which is to parade me to the various unmarried gentlemen she is inviting."

"But they could be ancient. Older than Papa even!"

"Quite so. I was beside myself wondering how I was to evade her little plan and now you have offered me the perfect solution."

"Then, we are both happy. Now, drink up Anthea, I must go home as soon as possible to let Papa know that I have engaged my very own chaperone. He will think me terribly clever for doing so – all on my own!"

Linette smiled as she put a forkful of cake into her delicate mouth and Anthea felt a thrill run through her.

The plan was a daring one and Anthea hoped that Linette's father would not present too many objections.

'After all,' she pondered, 'Linette has only just met me and she will not know if I was of good character. And what if she told him that I was running away? What if her father knows my stepmother?'

Brushing aside these worries, Anthea finished her tea and Linette paid for both of them.

'Italy!' she said to herself, as the two girls parted company. '*Naples!* I was so disappointed that we had to forgo our trip there in the summer and now I am to return.'

She could not wait to go home to begin plotting her escape. Even before the carriage had turned into Mount Street, she had planned to pack a trunk and hide it in one of the guest bedrooms.

'Stepmother shall not have her own way this time,' she thought, as she walked up the steps of the house. 'And if Papa thinks so little of me to allow me to be packed off with the first available man, he will not miss me at all.'

She could hardly wait to put her plan into motion as she ran upstairs – her head swimming with excitement and trepidation.

*

She was very much the dutiful daughter that week – even her stepmother remarked on the change in her.

"I am so glad that you are seeing things my way," she commented on the evening of the ball.

"If I suggest that a certain gentleman asks you to dance, then you should understand that you must make a very great impression upon him. I will expect you to be at your most charming and attractive. Is that clear?"

"Of course, Stepmother," answered Anthea, as the new maid busied herself around her.

Anthea was wearing her new gown from Monsieur Henri's and was suitably gratified when Lady Preston had pronounced that she looked 'utterly charming'.

Later, at the foot of the stairs, when her father first set eyes upon her, she could see them well up with tears and for a second a shadow of his old self flickered back.

"You look beautiful, Anthea," he sighed quietly.

Anthea moved to kiss him, but he turned away and moved smartly down the hall before she could do so.

It stung like a whiplash to have him snub her so.

But holding her head up and fixing a firm smile to her lips, she walked quickly into the drawing room.

The servants had cleared out the dining room and opened up the doors between it and the drawing room next door to create a huge ballroom.

Anthea could not recall the last time such a grand event had been held in the house.

As she was whirled around the room by one boring man after another, all Anthea could concentrate on was the trunk upstairs and her carpet bag for the journey ahead.

'The new maid is so dozy, she will not realise that half of my clothes have disappeared,' she said to herself, as Algernon Trotwood stood on her toes for the fourth time.

Algernon was about forty and one of the gentlemen that her stepmother had earmarked as a possible husband for her. He smelled of cobwebs and musty clothes and his hand was hot and clammy as he held hers.

And then there was Daniel Beauchamp – more her own age, being around twenty-eight, but who held her far too tightly during the polka and who wrenched her closer each time she tried to pull away.

At every stage she was aware of her stepmother's watchful gaze, so she smiled and chatted amiably, in spite of longing to run away and hide in her room.

As the orchestra struck up a waltz, Daniel clutched her to him as if he was drowning, and Anthea, feeling sick to her stomach, simply smiled.

'The sooner I get away from this house and these dreadful men, the better,' she murmured to herself.

'If I had any doubts at all about this wild plan, then tonight has made my mind up. Tomorrow I will slip away with Linette and I shall be on my way to Italy.'

As she smiled at that thought, Daniel Beauchamp was already rehearsing his proposal speech in his head –

CHAPTER THREE

The next morning although she was awake at half-past eight, Anthea lay in bed until almost eleven o'clock.

As she stared at the blue ceiling, she was filled with a mixture of anticipation and anxiety.

The ball had been a big success for her stepmother, although Anthea was a little disappointed that none of her friends had been able to attend.

Anthea's toes still hurt from Algernon Trotwood's clumsy exertions and she noticed that one of her big toes was quite bruised.

'Oh, bother,' she thought. 'I shall have to be extra careful not to drop any luggage on my foot if I want to be able to hurry along without hobbling.'

Dismissing her new maid, Anthea got up and went to check on the trunk that she had made two of the footmen take downstairs the day before.

She had told them that it contained old clothing and she wanted it removed to the coach house.

Tiptoeing gingerly along the corridor and down the backstairs, Anthea soon found herself in the rarely used guest quarters at the back of the house.

She was pleased to see her trunk by the door.

'Good,' she said to herself. 'Now all I have to do is to get Fricker and one of his footmen to carry it outside.'

She crept back to her bedroom via the backstairs, hoping that she would not bump into any of the servants.

'They will most likely still be clearing up after the ball,' she reckoned, as she slid back into her room.

Anthea could not wait for the day to pass.

She had a bath, dressed herself, and then made her way downstairs. Her stepmother was in the morning room and her face broke into a rare smile as Anthea entered.

"Ah, at last!" she simpered. "The belle of the ball has deigned to honour us with her presence."

It took Anthea a moment to realise that she was not being ironic but was genuinely happy to see her.

"Would you care for some coffee? Fricker has just brought in a fresh pot and I can ring for another cup."

"Yes, thank you," replied Anthea, sitting down in a chair near her with a wary air.

Lady Preston rose and pulled the servants' bell.

"How are you this morning?" she enquired.

"Quite well, thank you. A little fatigued. Algernon Trotwood is quite the clumsiest dancer ever."

"Yes, he is a little ungainly, but never mind him – so what impression did you gain of Daniel Beauchamp? A fine young man with a great deal of land and wealth. His estates in Suffolk are pretty extensive. He is not nobility, you understand, but his father is a Member of Parliament and he is a most eligible gentleman."

Anthea thought carefully before answering, because she did not wish to spoil her stepmother's good mood, as it could be beneficial to keep her that way.

"I like him well enough," she muttered.

"He was very taken with you! In fact he is having luncheon with us today. He was very insistent to see you again that I did not see the point in keeping him waiting."

"Oh," she answered, taking the cup Fricker had just handed to her.

"Do try and be a little more enthusiastic, Anthea."

"I am sorry, Stepmother, I must be more fatigued than I had at first believed."

"Then the coffee will restore you. Do change for luncheon, Anthea, the rose silk is most becoming on you."

Anthea thought quickly.

'The rose silk dress is in my trunk! Goodness me! What shall I say?'

She made a show of drinking her coffee before then replying,

"Stepmother, should I not wear the dress that was delivered yesterday morning from Monsieur Henri's? It is a very fashionable primrose-yellow silk with oyster lace."

"Excellent idea. The colour will suit you very well and it will flatter Mr. Beauchamp no end if he believes that you have made a special effort for him."

Inwardly Anthea sighed with relief.

"I shall ask Maisy to press it for you at once," said Lady Preston, rising again to ring for Fricker.

Anthea attempted a weak smile and sat in silence whilst her stepmother chattered about the evening's events.

She became uncharacteristically talkative and, after a while, Anthea sought to take her leave as there was the matter of her trunk to attend to.

"If you will excuse me now, Stepmother, I shall go upstairs and begin to get ready. I assume Mr. Beauchamp will be here at, what, half-past twelve?"

"Of course, my dear, and don't rush down until you hear the gong. A little anticipation will not harm him. Far from it – to keep him waiting will increase his ardour."

'Ugh!' thought Anthea. 'I shall have to swallow my true feelings and not give any hint of my distaste for him.'

Lady Preston yawned as Anthea rose to leave.

"Oh, you must excuse me. I do believe I shall have to have a nap after luncheon. Perhaps you would entertain Mr. Beauchamp for me?"

"Of course," responded Anthea, saving her grimace until she had closed the door behind her.

Before luncheon she wrote a note to Linette, asking her to meet her in the Mews behind the house at half-past nine that evening and handed it to Fricker, charging him to have it delivered at once.

"And don't breathe a word to my stepmother," she cautioned him. "And, there is a large trunk of old clothes downstairs, could you have it taken to the coach house?"

'Very good, miss," he smiled and she could tell that he was pleased to be in complicity with her.

'It is obvious that he does not care for Stepmother, either,' she thought gleefully as she closed the door.

She noticed that the box in which her primrose-silk dress had arrived was lying open on the bed.

'Maisy must have taken it to press it,' she thought with some satisfaction. 'I shall have to wear it this evening and put my cashmere coat over the top to keep me warm.'

Her bath was already run, so she jumped in, washed her hair and face, wondering what might lie ahead.

As Maisy was helping her dress, she heard the front door bell and Fricker answering it. Glancing at the clock, she noticed that Daniel was a few minutes early.

'He is very keen,' she sighed mournfully.

Five minutes later she descended the stairs slowly and entered the drawing room.

Daniel Beauchamp's face lit up as he saw her.

"Astonishing," he murmured, as he bent and kissed her hand. "You are even more beautiful than you were last night and I did not think it possible."

"The dress is so becoming," added her stepmother approvingly.

As they chatted for a while, Anthea was conscious of Daniel's hot eyes upon her. He made her feel distinctly uncomfortable.

When luncheon was finished, on cue Lady Preston made a great show of stifling a yawn and then, announced,

"Anthea, my dear, as I am so tired after last night's ball, would you mind if I disappeared upstairs for a little lie-down? Mr. Beauchamp, I am certain that I can leave you in my stepdaughter's capable hands."

With a ghastly smile she left them alone.

In the silence that followed, Daniel blurted out,

"I was thinking perhaps we might go for a walk."

"Of course," Anthea replied, ringing for Fricker. "I shall have our coats brought at once."

She and Daniel then emerged from the front door of Mount Street. The day was overcast and it looked as if rain was threatening.

Anthea was hoping that the heavens would open up shortly so that they could return home – and that Daniel would take the hint and leave.

"Perhaps a turn round Berkeley Square?" he asked, offering her his arm. She took it gingerly and tried not to allow him to pull her too close, as he had done the previous evening when they were dancing.

He was not at all a good-looking man – being short and round with a curious ginger moustache. His hair was a nondescript brown and his mouth drooped in a manner that reminded Anthea of a codfish.

'I do so hope that none of my friends see me,' she thought, rather uncharitably, 'it would be awful if someone was to see us together and assume we were intimate.'

She was hoping too that Fricker had remembered to have her trunk removed to the coach house.

Daniel then cut directly into her broodings.

"There is to be a large house party in Cheltenham next weekend, Anthea. Would you care to join me?"

Anthea stopped abruptly on the pavement. She had been so deep in thought that she had not been listening to a word that Daniel Beauchamp was saying.

He was regarding her with a quizzical expression – awaiting some kind of reply.

"Oh, I don't know," she replied after a little while. "Stepmother is always organising things for me to do and I shall have to ask her. May I write and let you know?"

"Of course," agreed Daniel, a little too eagerly.

They arrived at Berkeley Square dodging the many carriages hurtling around the area.

Anthea lifted her skirt, anxious that the wet should not soil the delicate silk.

'Oh, why did I not change?' she grumbled, as she noticed that a recent shower had made the green muddy.

Thankfully the pavements were dry as long as she walked in the middle of them.

Unfortunately this meant that Daniel was forced to walk closer to her side.

'I shall just have to put up with him,' she thought stoically, as they promenaded into the fashionable square.

"I was hoping that your father would be at home today," he remarked suddenly.

"Oh, Papa is always occupied with his business or is at his Club. We rarely see him during the day."

"I would wish to speak him in any case. When are you expecting him?"

"I have just remembered – he is at the races today. Usually we do not see him until very late as he often dines at his Club on race days."

Daniel's face fell and then, after thinking for a few moments, it lit up again.

"Do you know which Club he frequents?"

"Why, Boodles," replied Anthea, knowing full well that he was a member of the Carlton.

"Really? That is dashed bad luck as I was thrown out of there once. Perhaps I shall come back another day. Do you know if he will be at home tomorrow evening?"

"It is highly likely, although he is often not at home until after dinner."

Daniel nodded his head deep in thought.

'Goodness – is he going to ask for my hand?' said Anthea to herself. 'I am very glad that I will not be in the country! I feel sure he would track me down if I were.'

As they crossed Berkeley Square and into Curzon Street, Anthea attempted to take her arm out of his, but he squeezed his elbow inwards and trapped it.

'I cannot wait for us to reach home,' she mused, as she gave up trying to discreetly free herself from him.

Once back outside the front door of Mount Street, Anthea smiled and stretched out her hand.

"Well, thank you so much for the nice walk," she smiled, as sweetly as she could. "I hope that you will not think me rude, but I have so much to do this afternoon."

Daniel's face fell and he looked very disappointed.

"Of course. Do not forget to write and let me know if you are able to attend the house party in Cheltenham."

"I shall do my best," she answered.

Daniel then shook her hand before turning around smartly and walking away.

Anthea heaved a deep sigh of relief as he rounded the corner and felt elated that it would be a very long time before she set eyes on him again.

Fricker opened the door and she stepped inside.

"Is my stepmother up and about?" she asked, taking off her gloves and hat.

"Not yet, miss. She is still asleep."

"And my trunk?"

"In the coach house, miss."

"Thank you so very much, Fricker," she murmured, looking at him earnestly.

'Oh, I shall miss him almost as much as Papa,' she told herself as she ran lightly up the stairs.

Looking down she noticed mud on her dress.

'I shall have to ask Maisy to sponge this for me at once. I shall want to take it with me.'

She took it off and rang the bell. Maisy carried the garment away promising to bring it back in time for dinner.

Suddenly there was a knock on her door.

"Come in," Anthea called in her bright clear voice.

She was somewhat surprised to see her stepmother glide into the room.

"I am sorry I was not up when you came home," she said, seating herself in the armchair by the fireplace.

"Well then, did Daniel Beauchamp propose? I was expecting that he might from what he said last night."

Anthea sighed and tried not to burst out laughing as her stepmother's machinations were all so obvious!

"No, Stepmother, but he did seem quite anxious to see Papa. I told him he might find him at his Club later."

"Then, I shall go to my room at once and compose the announcement, for as soon as he has offered for you, I will place a notice in *The Times* so that everyone important will know of the engagement.

"I do hope that Mr. Beauchamp is not fond of long engagements – a December wedding would be so suitable. Perhaps, Christmas Eve?"

"Whatever you wish," replied Anthea, lowering her face. "Oh, look, here is Maisy with my gown. Did you remove the mud stains?"

"Yes, miss."

"Then, I shall put it on at once. I want Papa to see me in this dress. It is so pretty."

Satisfied that her plan was in motion, Lady Preston left the room. The smug expression on her face was enough to make Anthea giggle – for she knew that, in a few short hours, that smile would be wiped away when she had fled.

'Tonight cannot come quick enough,' she pondered as Maisy helped her into the yellow-silk dress. 'And the sooner, the better!'

*

Dinner was a quiet affair that evening.

Anthea was far too nervous to eat very much and fortunately her stepmother rather arrogantly attributed it to anxiety about Daniel's impending proposal.

"That is a lovely gown you are wearing," remarked her father, looking up from his soup. "Is it something you bought the other day in Bond Street?"

"Yes, Papa."

Looking at her Papa, she suddenly felt a sharp pain in her heart. Although he had not been his old self of late, she would really miss him.

'But I must not waiver,' she determined. 'My mind is made up and I have to leave. It is even more essential that I go now that Daniel Beauchamp has set his cap at me.

I could never endure an enforced engagement, let alone a marriage to *him* and that is what will happen if I stay.'

"Daniel Beauchamp was here for luncheon," Lady Preston interjected. "He wishes to speak with you."

"Ah-ha!" cried Sir Edward. "Is this, by any chance, the prelude to an *announcement*?"

He chuckled away to himself and made jokes on the subject with his wife, oblivious to the fact that Anthea was squirming in her chair.

She looked at the clock and it was nearly nine.

She quickly finished her pudding and then asked to be excused.

"I have a slight headache," she explained.

"You shouldn't gobble your food," commented her stepmother. "If you do not digest properly, of course, you will get headaches."

"Yes, Stepmother," she said rising from the table.

As she bid them goodnight, she saw that they were so wrapped up in each other that they were not taking any notice of her.

Casting one last lingering glance at her father, she felt tears pricking her eyes as she did not know when she might set eyes on him again.

'I will write to him before I leave,' she decided.

Once upstairs she rang for Maisy and said that she would not be required any more that evening.

"And have tomorrow off," she added, as the girl, bobbed a curtsy. "You have worked hard this weekend and I can manage perfectly well without you."

Maisy looked delighted as she left the room.

Anthea then locked the door and set about writing a note to her father.

'I must tell him not to worry. I will say that I am safe with a friend and that we are travelling. I shall not say where or when, otherwise he may attempt to find me.'

Again she felt a wave of sadness sweep over her as she folded the writing paper and addressed it to him.

She propped it up on her dressing table where she knew Maisy would find it and then finished putting the last few items she would need into her carpetbag.

'There,' she muttered to herself, as she snapped the clasp shut. 'Now I must put on my hat and coat and go downstairs. It is almost *time*.'

Taking her book from her bedside table, she slung her coat over her arm with her hat and bag beneath it.

'Then, if one of the servants sees me, I shall say I am going out for a walk to help clear my headache.'

She pulled the door open slowly, listening for signs of life – all she could hear was the ticking of the hall clock.

Holding her breath, she edged out onto the landing and then tiptoed towards the backstairs.

As she slowly descended, she was wondering how she could slip past the kitchen without being seen.

'Surely the servants will be eating in the servants' hall?' she surmised, as she reached the door that led to a passageway that would take her into the Mews outside.

She hesitated for a long moment.

Screwing up her courage, she turned the handle and crept out into the passage.

She was almost at the back door when suddenly a tall figure loomed in front of her.

"Miss Preston!"

It was Fricker.

Anthea stared at him, speechless with fright.

"I – I – "

"No need to explain, miss," he whispered. "It is our little secret. I have not seen you."

"Thank you very much, Fricker," breathed Anthea, touching the butler's cuff in a gesture of gratitude.

He opened the back door and looked about.

"There is a carriage waiting in the Mews – "

"Yes. Goodbye, Fricker, and thank you again."

"Good luck, miss."

She did not hesitate. She walked quickly into the Mews and then ran towards Linette's carriage.

Linette caught sight of her and waved.

Then as Anthea approached the open carriage door, Linette leaned forward and whispered,

"Shall I ask the footmen to load your bags? Where are they?"

"In the coach house. A large trunk by the door."

Linette gestured to the footmen and within minutes they were loading the trunk onto the rear of the carriage.

"Oooh, I am so terribly excited!" squealed Linette, throwing a cashmere blanket over Anthea's knees.

"I hope that you brought a coat otherwise you will be freezing. That's a lovely dress you are wearing, but it is not sufficiently warm to keep out the chill."

Anthea smiled.

"I have my coat here, but did not have time to put it on. I got caught sneaking out by our butler!"

"Will he – ?"

"No, he is a friend and will not say a thing. I can trust him with my life."

"Ready, my Lady?"

One of the footmen put his head into the travelling compartment.

"Yes, make all haste, Haskins. Papa is waiting for us at the Nelson Hotel. You know the way there?"

"Yes, my Lady, we have the Master's fastest horses and we shall be in Portsmouth before dawn."

"Good, and well done Haskins!" exclaimed Linette, squeezing Anthea's hand. "Oh, I am so excited! I cannot wait for you to meet Papa – he is already in Portsmouth."

"When does our ship sail?"

"On the morning tide. Papa is very particular about sailing promptly."

As the carriage moved off down the Mews, Anthea could not resist taking one last look at the house she had lived in all her life.

'When will I set foot inside again?' she wondered. 'Oh, *what have I done*?'

In spite of all her excitement and knowing that what she was doing was the only way she would find a life of her own, Anthea could not help crying.

Two large tears were trickling down her cheeks as she pressed her face up against the window as the carriage picked up speed.

"*Goodbye*, Papa!" she whispered. "I will always love you."

CHAPTER FOUR

Anthea did her level best to avoid Linette seeing her cry – she did not want her to feel guilty or awkward.

'Besides, she is just a girl and I am supposed to be looking after her – she is not here to be *my* comforter!'

The carriage had a very luxurious interior, the seats were well sprung and covered in cashmere blankets while the backs were leather and buttoned.

Although her father's best carriage was considered expensive, the Earl's put his into the shade.

Anthea snuggled up beneath the blankets and tried to close her eyes.

'Why is it I feel as if my heart is being torn from my chest?' she wondered. 'Can leaving Papa really be such a wrench after how little concern he has shown me of late? I find it hard to forgive him for keeping me in the dark over his marriage and for not honouring Mama's memory with a better choice of new wife.'

Although she would not care to admit it, Anthea's view of love had been considerably tainted by her dreadful experience with Jolyon Burnside.

Since he had jilted her, she had not even so much as looked at a young man in a romantic way.

'My heart is closed to that side of life,' she mused. 'Perhaps becoming a chaperone will help ease the pain of my loneliness. Linette is a lively girl and if this trip goes well, maybe she will ask me to accompany her on another.

I can think of less pleasant occupations in life – and, until Papa comes to his senses, I cannot return to Mount Street.'

Eventually her fatigue won and she fell asleep.

She slumbered soundly, only being shaken awake when the carriage clattered over a wooden bridge.

She opened her eyes with a jolt and at once felt ill. Her mouth was dry and the rocking motion of the carriage made her nauseous.

Outside the sky was beginning to lighten and a few seagulls scudded overhead.

"Where are we?" yawned Linette loudly. "Are we in Portsmouth yet?"

"I do believe we are almost there."

"How exciting! Wait until you see Papa's ship – it is modern and the height of luxury. If someone blindfolded you and took you on board without telling you where you were, you would think you were in the best hotel!"

"It sounds wonderful," agreed Anthea.

"And the crew on-board are so handsome! Captain MacFarlane always looks after me beautifully and they all make a big fuss of me. They will be delighted to meet you and you will enjoy the trip a great deal."

Anthea smiled as Linette bubbled over with girlish enthusiasm.

She thought her rather young for her age as when she herself had been twenty, she was already engaged to Jolyon Burnside and contemplating marriage.

She could no sooner imagine Linette married than she could see her flying to the moon. For despite the fact that her father was an Earl with an international business, Linette was quite the innocent.

"Look! I see a ship's mast!" cried Linette, pointing out of the window.

Anthea squinted and could just make out something poking above the buildings in front of them.

A little later after moving slowly through crowded streets, the carriage pulled up at the quayside in front of a gleaming steamship.

Anthea could see the words '*The Sea Sprite*' on the prow.

"There it is! Look!"

Linette was obviously immensely proud of the ship and could not wait to show it off to her.

"I do hope Papa is already on board. I have hardly seen him these past few weeks."

She had run down the steps of the carriage before Anthea could reply.

She smiled to herself and followed her out onto the quayside. The footmen were busy unloading their luggage. She noticed that Linette had a great many trunks and cases while she had just one.

As she watched the activity on the quayside, Linette was already running up the gangway.

'She is so thrilled to be seeing her father,' thought Anthea wistfully. 'How I miss mine already.'

Slowly she walked over towards the ship and up to the gangway.

The salty air whipped at her face and breathing it in made her feel a great deal more cheerful.

"Come and meet our Captain MacFarlane," called out Linette, waving at her from the deck.

Next to her stood a tall handsome man in uniform who saluted as Anthea drew level with him.

"Captain, this is my new friend and my chaperone – Miss Anthea Preston."

"Welcome, Miss Preston," he smiled. "I hope that you will enjoy the voyage. Now would you mind stepping to one side as my men are bringing the luggage on board."

"Oh, goodness. Did I really pack as much as that?" cried out Linette looking horrified, "and you only have the one trunk!"

"I confess, I am a little worried that I will not have enough clothes for the journey," answered Anthea, as she watched the two sailors struggling with an enormous trunk.

"Oh, nonsense. If you run out of gowns, you can wear some of mine. We are about the same size, I would guess. Now, come along – the Captain says Papa is not on board yet, but I want you to come and see the Saloon."

She took Anthea's hand and led her along the deck to a pair of doors.

"In here!" she exploded.

As she promised the Saloon was most luxurious.

There were sofas, bookcases full of bound volumes, a piano and a *chaise longue* smothered with cushions. On the floor were Turkish rugs and fine paintings on the walls.

"It looks *so* wonderful," remarked Anthea, looking around her. "Did your father choose the art?"

"Oh, yes. Papa loves art, but he says that he never has sufficient time to indulge himself. When we arrive in Naples, I want to surprise him and find him something new for this room. Will you help me?"

"Of course, I should like that very much. I hear that there are plenty of artists living in the area and we might happen across the next Botticelli or Leonardo!"

"Wouldn't that just be divine? Now where is Papa? He is very naughty for not being here when we arrived."

Linette stamped her foot impatiently and pouted.

Just then the Captain came into the Saloon with a member of his crew dressed in a white jacket.

"Ladies, this is Jackson. He is to be your Steward for the voyage and he will see to your every comfort. You must not be afraid to ask him for whatever you desire."

"Breakfast now would be just perfect," suggested Linette, throwing herself down on the *chaise*.

"I shall see what chef can make for you, my Lady."

Half an hour later, Jackson appeared with a buffet trolley of rolls, fruit and a huge tureen full of kedgeree.

"Thank you so very much," smiled Linette, as she helped herself to a peach. "Jackson, when do we sail?"

"Quite soon," he answered.

Just as he spoke there was a commotion on deck.

"Papa!" exclaimed Linette, jumping up.

Before she reached the door, a tall handsome man with dark hair and startling amber eyes strode in.

"Darling," he called out, as Linette threw her arms round his neck and kissed him on the cheek.

"I am so sorry that I was not here when you arrived. I am afraid I was detained."

"You are here now, Papa, and I want you to meet my new friend. This is Miss Anthea Preston. Anthea, this is my Papa."

Anthea walked towards him and was immediately struck at how young he was.

'He can be no more than ten or twelve years older than I am,' she thought. 'He must have had Linette when he was very young. And Linette does not take after him in looks in the least – she must resemble her mother.'

"I am delighted to meet you," said the Earl, taking Anthea's hand and shaking it warmly.

"Anthea is my new chaperone and I found her all by myself. Isn't that clever of me to find a replacement for Mrs. Catherall?"

"You never cease to amaze me," answered the Earl, smiling indulgently at her. "I hope you will enjoy the trip, Miss Preston, *The Sea Sprite* is one of the swiftest ships on the ocean and you will be in Naples by today next week."

"But you are coming too, aren't you, Papa?"

"Oh, I am afraid I will not be sailing with you, my dearest," he sighed. "There have been some problems with a ship we are building in Southampton for a Greek Prince. I will have to go there to resolve the matter first and will be following in another ship. I will meet you in Naples."

"*Oh, Papa!*"

"I am so sorry, Linette, but it cannot be avoided. You will not miss me with Miss Preston here to keep you company."

Anthea found it hard not to stare at the Earl – there was something of Prince Albert about his elegant features and his bearing was almost as regal.

He was so tall with broad shoulders and a muscular physique. He had the air of a man who was fond of the outdoor life and all its pursuits, rather than living the soft life of an idle aristocrat.

Anthea thought it strange that their paths had not crossed before in London. Her mother and father had been the toast of Southampton at one time and knew most of the important shipbuilding families.

Without being summoned, Jackson brought in some more tea and they sat and drank chatting merrily.

Anthea had not realised how famished she was and, without wishing to appear greedy, ate with relish all she could from the delicious buffet, all the time regarding the Earl closely as he talked about his business in Naples.

'I cannot believe that this is Linette's *father*!' she said to herself, unable to stop staring at him. 'If I had met him at a ball or party, I would have taken him for a single gentleman, not someone with a grown-up daughter!'

The Earl then returned her gaze and smiled at her. Immediately she felt a flush rising in her face and chest.

Quickly she looked down and examined her nails.

'I have never seen such unusual eyes,' she mused to herself. 'They are like pieces of polished amber.'

She glanced at Linette's animated face and tried to detect some likeness to her father there, but she could not find one solitary feature in common.

As she did so the Earl rose and turned to her.

"I must thank you so much for coming to the rescue of my daughter," he said with a dazzling smile. "Although she is perfectly safe on board *The Sea Sprite*, I shall feel much easier knowing that she has a companion – and such a charming one at that."

Anthea blushed once more and scolded herself for being unable to offer an equally flattering response.

'I am behaving like a tongue-tied child.'

"Tell me," continued the Earl. "Do you and your family live in London?"

"Y-yes, my Lord," she stammered, falling over her words. "My Mama died a few years ago – but Papa still resides in Mount Street."

"Ah, I know it well, you must be neighbours of the Comte de Chantilly? He has a house at the end of the street, I believe."

"Yes, my Lord, I have often seen him and his wife in their carriage. Although I do not count them as friends, they are certainly acquaintances."

"And do the Helfonds still reside at number 16?"

"No, they moved in April – Sir Albert was sent to India on Government Business. I was sad to see them go, as I was very fond of their daughter Elspeth. She is now married and living in Bristol."

The Earl's face darkened.

"India?" he murmured. "I hope that he remains safe and sound – it can be a treacherous place to live with the Russians constantly knocking on the door."

Something about his expression warned Anthea not to pursue the topic of conversation. It was as if a shadow had passed over his face.

"Now, I must take my leave, dearest," he turned to Linette. "I must travel to Southampton and try to placate Prince Aristos and ensure that his ship is delivered on time. Miss Preston, it was a pleasure to meet you and I look forward to renewing our acquaintance in Italy."

He brushed past Anthea and picked up his hat from the table near her elbow.

Even though it was just for a fleeting second, it was as if she had been touched by fire.

"Thank you for looking after Linette," he said in a low voice, as his amber gaze bore into Anthea's eyes. "I shall make certain that whatever you desire is yours."

A shiver ran through Anthea's body.

He had somehow loaded his words with meaning – a meaning she could only dare to guess at.

She felt that he was making it plain that he found her attractive, but she was too uncertain of herself to really believe her instincts.

"You never stay long enough, Papa," complained Linette, kissing him and breaking the spell.

"We shall have plenty of time together in Naples. I hope you have a pleasant voyage and I know that Captain MacFarlane will do his utmost for you."

He threw Anthea one last lingering look and left.

"Is he not handsome?" remarked Linette, as soon as he was out of earshot. "Lots of ladies have lost their hearts to him, but he has never re-married. What is more, he does not appear the least bit interested in finding a new wife.

"I should really like a stepmother as I am very often lonely when Papa is away working. And I am certain that not all stepmothers are as horrible as you say yours is!"

Anthea laughed.

"I was, I am afraid, unlucky, but tell me, when did your mother pass away, Linette?"

"Ages ago. She died when I was an infant. I do not even have her photograph. Papa does not talk about her."

"You must take after your mother in appearance as your Papa is so different to you."

"That is what everyone says, but Papa did say once that I resembled my Mama. She was Scottish, you know. Grandfather has an estate up in Scotland and I believe that was where Papa met Mama. I wish I knew more about her – it is terrible not to know where you come from and not to be in contact with half of your family."

"You don't ever hear from your Scottish relatives?"

"Not a word. Grandma Hayworth, Papa's mother, once let slip something about '*those awful McGregors*' and that led me to believe there had been a quarrel many years ago and all contact with Mama's family has been cut off as a result."

"How terrible for you," breathed Anthea.

"Yes, it is a real bore. Grandma Hayworth is such a grump. She always looks at me in a disapproving fashion."

Anthea was just pondering the intriguing story and the mystery of the Earl's marriage when Jackson came in.

"My Lady, Miss Preston – your cabins are ready for you. Would you care to follow me?"

"I hope we are not below deck," muttered Linette, as she skipped towards the door.

"We would not dare," answered Jackson. "You are on this level and your cabins are next door to each other."

He led them along the deck to the port side of the ship, where the guest cabins were located.

"You are to be in his Lordship's cabin, my Lady, and Miss Preston is in the one you usually occupy."

"The one with the connecting doors?"

Jackson nodded.

"How wonderful! Anthea, it's such fun being able to enter each other's cabins without going out on deck."

Jackson showed Anthea to her cabin.

Her trunk was already unpacked and everything had been put into a mahogany wardrobe against the wall. At the far end of the cabin was a double-sized bed made up with fresh white linen and topped with a red satin quilt that was exactly the same shade as the luxurious Axminster carpet.

The walls were papered with lovely wall coverings in a *fleur-de-lys* pattern and hung with well-chosen works of art depicting marine scenes.

"Thank you," she gasped, "this cabin is delightful."

"Look here!" cried out Linette, bursting through the connecting doors. "Isn't this just divine? Have you found the bathroom yet? It's all so very modern."

She went to a door along the wall and opened it.

"See? You will have to ask Jackson to fill the bath for you, but this is a great luxury on board. Papa does not believe in stinting anything and that is why his ships are in demand all over the world. Most of the crowned heads of Europe boast a Hayworth ship."

"Your Papa must be very clever to be able to sell ships to other countries that have shipbuilding industries of their own."

"Oh, yes. In fact, I know that there is at least one in Naples hopping mad that Papa seems set to snatch a very important commission from under their noses. But we all know that British ships are the best in the world!"

"Naturally," agreed Anthea.

Just then the roar of engines under their feet and a shuddering motion alerted them that the ship was moving.

"We are on our way!" exclaimed Linette excitedly. "Shall we go on deck and watch the English coast vanish behind us? I do always so love to wave it goodbye. Then we can come back to change as it will not be long before luncheon is served."

She grasped Anthea by the hand and dragged her outside onto the deck.

A blast from the ship's horn made them both jump and smoke from the funnels belched out, almost obscuring the sun.

"Goodbye England!" waved Linette cheerily.

She was so absorbed that she did not notice Anthea standing behind her, quietly shedding tears.

'Goodbye to you England,' she wept silently, 'and who knows what will lie in wait for me across the sea, but whatever it is, I must welcome it for there is now no going back.'

CHAPTER FIVE

The first day at sea was a very enjoyable experience for both Anthea and Linette.

First Captain MacFarlane showed Anthea round the ship. She found it thrilling to stand on the bridge and view all the various instruments.

"It is one of the most modern ships afloat," boasted the Captain proudly. "And one of the swiftest."

"It is the first time that I have been on a steamship," added Anthea. "I have only ever sailed on yachts before."

"You will find a great difference between the two as we are not dependent upon the wind," answered Captain MacFarlane. "And we can reach a far greater speed."

He took her and Linette below decks and showed them the engine room. The noise and heat were incredible and Anthea felt quite faint.

By the time they had ended their tour Jackson came to find them to announce that luncheon was ready.

They made their way to the Saloon to find a buffet of lobster, tunny fish and cold meats spread out along with a variety of rice dishes.

"Such fabulous food," exclaimed Anthea. "I can see that we are going to be very spoilt on this voyage."

"Papa is so accustomed to the best of everything," replied Linette, loading her plate with lobster. "He is very fussy about what he eats."

"Will he have time in Naples to show us around?" asked Anthea hopefully.

She was keen to spend more time with the dashing Earl.

"Oh, I expect he will take us to dinner, but he will not come sightseeing with us – his business commitments will ensure that."

'What a pity,' thought Anthea, although she did not voice her disappointment.

After an afternoon nap the two girls had great fun chatting and becoming better acquainted.

They spent some time in the Saloon where Anthea played the piano for Linette.

"You are really very clever," sighed Linette, as the last bars of a piece by Brahms faded. "I am all fingers and thumbs when I try to learn to play and in the end my music teacher gave up on me."

"I am not that good really, I just play passably well. Mama was the one who was a brilliant pianist. Papa used to say that she could have played with any orchestra."

Their conversation was interrupted by the Captain entering the Saloon.

"Excuse me, my Lady," he said, addressing Linette. "Dinner will be in one hour. I also thought I should alert you both that we shall be rounding the Bay of Biscay later this evening."

"Oh, is that bad?" enquired Anthea, worried by his stern countenance.

"It will more than likely be pretty rough. The Bay of Biscay is notorious for its cross currents and, as a result, we can expect a heavy swell."

"He means we might be seasick," giggled Linette.

"That is correct, my Lady, but we do have a ship's doctor should either of you feel unwell."

"That is most reassuring," added Anthea, getting up and wandering over to the porthole.

She looked out and the sea outside looked as clear and calm as glass.

With the sun shining so brightly and just a gentle breeze, it was hard to imagine the ship rolling around.

'And this ship is heavy and sturdy compared with a yacht,' she reflected. 'I cannot believe that we should feel the ship pitching even if we do hit rough seas.'

However a few hours later after dinner, Anthea was to discover that her theory did not hold good.

Around midnight the ship began to roll alarmingly and she suddenly felt quite unwell.

Taking herself off to bed, she awoke in the middle of the night and was very sick indeed.

All through the next day and the day after, both she and Linette were confined to their cabins.

"Oh, I do feel so ill," groaned Linette, as the ship's doctor came to call on them.

Anthea did not want to even open her mouth in case she was sick again. The doctor attempted to give her some medicine to calm her stomach, but she could not face it.

*

Eventually two days later they moved further down the coast of France and the seas became calmer once more.

That afternoon Anthea did feel well enough to get out of bed and sit in an armchair.

Jackson brought her some weak tea and dry toast.

"Thank you, Jackson. Is Lady Linette up yet?"

"She is still asleep. I will look in on her presently."

"Where do we dock next?"

"Marseilles, miss. We always dock there for a few days in order to take on more supplies and fuel."

As Anthea chewed on her toast, she thought, as she had done constantly over the past few days, of the Earl.

It had been a long time since a man had aroused her interest – and certainly she had felt no romantic attachment to anyone since Jolyon Burnside.

'But could I trust him with my heart?' she thought. 'I know so little about him or his involvements. Although Linette professes not to have seen any sweethearts, he may be the sort of man who keeps his private life to himself.

'For all I know, he may have a string of *amours* all over Europe. He must have the opportunity, as he travels so often – and he is such a handsome man, as Linette says, and it is no surprise that women yearn to ensnare him.'

She was still ruminating on the Earl when Linette came stumbling in through the connecting doors.

"So, you are up as well?" she yawned, rubbing her stomach. "Goodness, I didn't think it possible to feel so ill. Usually I have good sea legs and am never seasick."

"It has been very rough for the past few days."

"Unusually so," Linette replied, sitting gingerly on a chair. "My stomach feels better than it did, but oh, how it aches!"

"Jackson said that we are docking in Marseilles for a day or so. I will welcome having dry land underneath my feet again."

"Quite so. Have you visited Marseilles before?"

"No, Linette. I did not venture South when I was in France."

"It is a most interesting place. Papa never allows me out on my own there, but I do not think I would care to walk the streets without a gentleman with me."

"Is it dangerous?"

"It is a little, mostly around the port. Papa says that with all the taverns and drinking dens it is not a safe place for young women to frequent. If we do go ashore, I should imagine that the Captain would give us an escort. Oh, I do hope we get Midshipman Norton – he is most amusing."

*

The next few days passed quickly.

The sun shone and the sea was not too rough, so the two girls made the most of sunbathing and relaxing.

And finally they arrived in Marseilles on a baking-hot September day.

"Goodness! It's so hot!" groaned Anthea. "I had not expected it to be so warm."

"Oh, yes," replied Linette. "It is often over eighty degrees in September. So you will definitely not need your cashmere coat in Marseilles."

"Excuse me, my Lady, but the Captain asked me to come and make myself known to you. I am Midshipman Jones and I will be escorting you ashore."

Linette looked up from her deckchair and regarded the tall young man closely. He was attractive in a rather girlish way with his jet-black hair and pale-blue eyes and his features were small and regular.

"Where is Midshipman Norton?"

"He is with the Captain on the bridge."

Linette pouted as she always did when something displeased her. Anthea, a little embarrassed on behalf of the Midshipman, smiled at him.

"I don't know Marseilles, what do you recommend we see?"

"There are many interesting shops, Miss Preston,"

he answered her gratefully. "And fine cafes. You should really try *bouillabaisse* while you are there."

"That is a local dish, is it not?"

"Yes, miss. A kind of hearty fish stew. If you do not care for garlic and onions, however, you may not find it to your taste."

"Oh, I am very fond of them. I have been to France on many occasions and went to Finishing School in Paris. One of the highlights was the wonderful French food."

"Then it is settled. I just happen to know the perfect café tucked away in the back streets that most tourists do not know. As you speak French, you will have no problem as the staff don't speak a word of English."

"I shall look forward to it."

Midshipman Jones bowed and then turned smartly on his heel and strode off down the deck.

"Ooh, I think you have an admirer," teased Linette. "He seemed terribly impressed with the fact that you could speak French!"

"Nonsense," replied Anthea. "He is just a very nice young man who was making polite conversation."

"You and I are alike, are we not? We do not set great store by romance."

"It was not always like that. I was once engaged to be married."

Linette sat up, her eyes inquisitive.

"Really? What happened?"

"He jilted me. He ran off with some woman he had met in France and they were married before I knew it."

"How terrible! You must have been crushed."

"Yes, I was. I have not so much as looked at any man since – "

Her voice trailed off.

She felt rather guilty for deceiving Linette. It was not a huge lie, but she also could not deny that the image of her father constantly occupied her thoughts.

He had awakened something inside her – something tender and frightening at the same time.

'The more I am occupied, the less I will then dwell on this ridiculous infatuation I seem to have fostered,' she said to herself, as she and Linette packed up their things to go below decks.

"I am excited about seeing Marseilles," remarked Linette, as they walked towards their cabin. "It seems like ages since I last felt the earth under my feet, much as I like being at sea, I do long for solid ground."

"I could not agree more. I hope, too, that we do not encounter any more rough seas – all my gowns are feeling loose as I have lost so much weight!"

An hour later they were both climbing into an open carriage that had been hired for their tour round Marseilles.

Midshipman Jones helped them into their seats and then sat down opposite Anthea.

"What a busy port," she commented.

"It seems to get more so each time I visit," replied Linette. "And the smell!"

She wrinkled her nose and then Midshipman Jones laughed.

"All kinds of cargo arrives here in Marseilles and not all of it fragrant spices or perfumes from Arabia," he informed them.

"My Papa much prefers the smell of engine oil and molten steel!" added Linette with a mocking smile. "I am more interested in the lovely perfumes from the South of France. Have you ever visited the jasmine fields of Grasse, Anthea?"

"No, I have never been this far South, although I hear there are wonderful lavender fields back at home in Norfolk and also in Hertfordshire."

"Really?"

"Oh, yes. Just outside the town of Hitchin there are many lavender fields. The apothecary in the Town Centre sells all kinds of fragrant products, soaps and the like."

"Then, I must endeavour to visit Hitchin," declared Linette. "I am quite fond of the scent of lavender."

"I prefer jasmine, although I have indulged in it. I was in mourning for so long, I felt it would be disrespectful to Mama to wear scent."

"And not so ladylike, either, Papa says only women of dubious character wear perfume – what do you think, Anthea?"

"I think that your Papa is a little harsh," she replied, thinking of how her Mama enjoyed Parma Violet perfume.

Midshipman Jones did his best to entertain his two charges. He showed them around the old part of the town and they visited a few galleries.

Then, he took them to a café and treated them to the famous *bouillabaisse*.

Anthea was thrilled by the checked tablecloths and the *patron* brought them all kind of tasty fare to sample.

The young waiter who served them took a bit of a shine to Linette, but did make it a bit obvious, much to her distress.

"He is only flirting with you, he means no offence," soothed Anthea, as she translated a compliment that he had made about Linette.

"I don't care for his attentions," responded Linette, stiffly. She was sitting upright in her chair with an anxious expression.

"I don't think he would harm you in any way, my Lady," interjected Midshipman Jones. "Especially as I am here to look after you."

"Papa would not like it!" snapped Linette, looking flustered and frightened.

The whole table fell silent and Anthea beckoned the *patron* and conversed with him in French. He was so taken aback that this English lady could speak his language that far from being offended that she had asked him if someone else might wait on the table, he sent them some delicious crème caramels for pudding by way of apology.

Anthea saw that Linette coloured as she explained to her why he had sent the puddings, but she did not make any comment.

"Goodness! I really don't think I could eat another morsel," sighed Anthea, after she had thanked the *patron* profusely for his largesse.

"We must eat every bit otherwise he might be upset with us," said Linette with a serious expression. She took up her spoon and dipped it into the creamy concoction.

'It's the little waiter who is upset,' thought Anthea, as she glanced over to where the sullen young man stood moping behind the small bar, not comprehending what he had done wrong.

For him and all Frenchmen, it was second nature to compliment a beautiful woman.

Later, after numerous cups of coffee, they left the café, but Anthea could not help but feel a little embarrassed at Linette's behaviour.

'She is young and naïve about men, it is true. But it seems she believes that strangers are out to gain something from her. I wonder what happened to make her frightened of them? Or maybe it is just that the Earl is very strict with her – in the absence of a wife. Linette might be the closest person to him and he does not want to lose her.'

They climbed back into their carriage and resumed their tour of the town and after a while Midshipman Jones advised that they should return to *The Sea Sprite*.

"Oh, but there is still so much we have not seen," grumbled Linette.

"I am sorry, my Lady. But as you well know, it is not safe for ladies to be out after dark in Marseilles. And you don't want to be late for dinner, do you?"

Although she had eaten a hearty lunch, Linette was fast becoming hungry again.

"No and the chef has promised lobster for tonight!"

In the carriage on the way back Anthea was so busy looking at the sights around her, that she did not notice that Midshipman Jones was gazing adoringly at her.

When they were back on board, he saluted her and then lingered before he took his leave of them.

Once he was out of earshot, Linette nudged her.

"He likes you. It's so obvious!"

"Ssh, Linette. You must not talk like that," replied Anthea colouring.

"He is so adorable! Like a little puppy with those big blue eyes."

"Except puppies do not have blue eyes," countered Anthea. "Besides, he is much younger than I am."

"Yes, there is that, I suppose," answered Linette, as she opened her cabin door. "A man should always be older than his sweetheart, do you not think?"

"That is the way of things."

Anthea took the opportunity, as they were on the subject, to raise the matter of Linette's fear of strange men.

"Linette, have you never had a sweetheart?" she asked, sitting down on her bed.

"No. I find the way that most men approach one rather intimidating."

"Such as that waiter this afternoon?"

"Precisely."

"But he only wished to flatter you in the way that French men are wont."

"I don't care for such advances," snapped Linette.

"But you have said that you are often called upon to entertain your father's clients – you must have had one of them flirt with you or pay you compliments."

"They do not dare!" replied Linette, with her eyes flashing. "Papa makes certain that they are courteous and respectful."

Anthea sensed that there was more to this than met the eye, but she did not wish to provoke or upset Linette, and so she excused herself and returned to her cabin.

'I can see that I shall have to tread carefully if I am to get to the bottom of this mystery,' she said to herself, as she arranged her hair for dinner, 'and I really must discover more about her father.'

*

The Sea Sprite left Marseilles the next day after the crew had replenished stocks and loaded more fuel.

Linette was so thrilled that several large fat lobsters still alive in buckets were brought on board.

Meanwhile she was much amused by the fact that Midshipman Jones appeared at every opportunity and was clearly smitten with Anthea.

"Has he declared himself yet?" she asked, as they reclined on their deckchairs one afternoon.

"Hush," answered Anthea. "He is simply doing his job and taking care of us."

"But we have Jackson for that. Midshipman Jones is more important than a Steward, yet he brings us drinks and nice things to eat all the time."

Anthea did not reply – she was thinking about how, the previous evening, he had slipped a volume of poetry under her cabin door along with a note asking her to read a particular verse.

When she had found it, she blushed to the roots of her hair as it was a love poem.

'Goodness! I shall have to nip this one in the bud,' she murmured to herself.

"I wonder if he will come to the Saloon after dinner again, as he did last night," queried Linette, "I must say he was very amusing and has a fine singing voice."

Later that evening, after they had eaten their dinner, Midshipman Jones did, indeed, come to the Saloon.

He was looking exceedingly smart and had taken a great deal of care with his personal appearance.

"Good evening, ladies," he began. "Miss Preston, would you care to walk out on deck with me? There is a wonderful constellation in the skies this evening that is so rarely glimpsed and I feel you should see it."

Linette stifled a giggle.

"I would love to," agreed Anthea, rising from her chair, throwing Linette a warning look and said she would see her presently.

Outside the evening was fine and warm.

The sky overhead was incredibly clear and the stars seemed to be closer to the earth than normal.

Midshipman Jones led Anthea to the top deck and pointed out the constellation to her.

"Can you see it? It is next to the Scales."

"Oh, where might they be?"

He moved behind Anthea and gently guided her in the right direction.

"Over there," he whispered in her ear.

Anthea suddenly felt a bit uncomfortable. Although he had moved away, he was still a presence behind her.

At last she saw it.

"How wonderful – and so bright! The stars do not shine so in England."

"That is because the sky is so much clearer here."

She turned to face him and, as she did so, she drew back.

His face was so full of adoration that she was not certain what he might do next.

He grasped her hand and kissed it.

"*Midshipman*!" she reacted strongly taking it away.

"Oh, I am so sorry but I am dying of love for you!" he declared, falling to his knees. "I cannot sleep or eat for thinking of you. Might I hope that you could maybe think of me favourably?"

Anthea stared at him for a moment not quite certain how to respond.

'He's just a boy compared to the Earl,' she thought. 'Even though he is attractive and kind, I could not possibly consider him as a suitor.'

Midshipman Jones remained on his knees, looking pleadingly up at her.

Eventually she spoke to him as gently as she could.

"Midshipman Jones, you really flatter me with your affections, but I am devoted to Linette and have promised her father that I shall concentrate on her and nothing else. I am sorry, but I am too busy to consider romance."

The deflated Midshipman rose to his feet slowly.

"I have made a perfect fool of myself," he sighed, hanging his head.

"Not at all. Shall we return to the Saloon? Linette will be getting restless."

"I should return to the bridge," he replied. "I take over the next watch presently and I should go and see what is happening."

He then saluted and strode off down the deck.

'What a to-do!' murmured Anthea, as she walked back to the Saloon. 'I had feared he was going to make a declaration and now the poor boy is crushed. How could I tell him that my attention is occupied by another?'

It was not Linette but *the Earl*.

His amber eyes haunted all her dreams and she so longed to see him again.

That evening the Captain said he expected to be in Naples in two days and now Anthea could not wait.

'I hope that the Earl's ship has overtaken ours and is already there,' she brooded, as she entered the Saloon.

"Anthea, did he try to kiss you?" demanded Linette.

She was relieved that the Captain was no longer in the room.

"Thankfully, no," she answered, sitting down with a sigh. "But he did say that he loved me."

"How exciting! What did you say to him?"

"I let him down as lightly as I could."

"Poor soul! Was he upset? I notice he is no longer with you. Did he run away?"

"He has returned to his post on the bridge and yes, he did seem rather unhappy."

"*Poor lovesick Midshipman Jones!*" sang Linette, twirling around the room.

She was still dancing when Jackson came to clear the glasses and coffee cups.

*

The very next day, Anthea was awakened early by Jackson carrying a letter for her.

"What is this?" she asked, rubbing her eyes.

"It's a telegraph message from his Lordship."

She took it eagerly and scanned it quickly.

"*I hope my daughter is behaving,*" it read. "*And I will see you both in Naples on Thursday. Looking forward to our reunion.*

Regards, Elliot Hayworth."

Anthea's heart was beating so fast that she thought she might swoon. She realised that it had not really been necessary for him to send a message – they had long since arranged that they would meet in Naples.

'Could I dare believe he has some feelings for me?' she thought with a mounting excitement. 'Why else would he send the message to me and not to Linette?'

Anthea tried to stay calm as she dressed, but then, totally unable to contain herself, as soon as she entered the Saloon, she blurted out to Linette that she had heard from the Earl.

"Papa telegraphed *you* and not *me*?" she pouted.

"I am certain he meant the telegram for both of us," she replied hastily.

"That will be it," nodded Linette, satisfied that she was right.

"I look forward to becoming better acquainted with your father," volunteered Anthea, as casually as she could. "He seems such an interesting gentleman, even if he is a bit of a mystery."

"What makes you say that?"

"I mean the fact that he has never remarried. When did you say your mother died?"

"Oh, I was only two. Mama miscarried and it was later that she succumbed to an internal infection. Papa does not like to talk about it."

"That is so tragic, it must have been awful for him," persisted Anthea. "Eighteen years is a long time for him to be on his own. Have there *never* been ladies in his life?"

"Not Papa!" answered Linette, laughing. "I am not even certain that he cares for romance. If he has romances, he keeps them to himself. I know he would never bring a lady into the house unless she was to be his wife – and that has never happened."

"That is a great pity. A man should not be without a woman."

"I agree, but Papa will never discuss such a subject with me."

Anthea fell silent.

She was still singing inside with joy at receiving his telegram and her lonely heart reached out to his, wherever he might be.

As the ship ploughed on towards Naples, she went up on deck after breakfast and gazed into the distance as the spray flew up into her face.

'I shall find a way into his heart,' she vowed to herself resolutely. 'Once we reach Naples, *I shall find a way.*'

CHAPTER SIX

As promised, *The Sea Sprite* duly arrived at Naples the following morning.

As the ship sailed majestically into its wide curving bay, Anthea was entranced by all she could see.

Above them towered Mount Vesuvius.

"Goodness, I hope it does not decide to erupt while we are here!" muttered Linette.

"Captain MacFarlane says it last erupted ten years ago. Although that was not a major eruption, many people were killed and the sea level was raised as a result."

"Oh, dear. Then, perhaps we shall be fortunate and it will remain intact whilst we are here, but look, there is smoke coming from it."

"That is because it is an active volcano. I have read a little about volcanoes after that dreadful eruption in Java that killed so many Dutch settlers as well as natives."

"Oh, yes. My Governess told me about it – it made me quite terrified of volcanoes for months. It was all she could do to reassure me that there were not any in Surrey!"

"That is where your home is?"

"That and the house in Scotland. Papa also keeps a house in Mayfair, although we don't go there much. Papa prefers the quiet life and enjoys hunting and riding."

"I didn't know you had a house so close to mine."

"Your family lives in Mayfair, Anthea?"

"Yes, in Mount Street."

"Oh, we are on Park Lane. Papa is never one for socialising or balls or *soirees*, although his lady admirers often invite him to them."

Anthea was silent as the ship slid into the dock.

'Very soon I shall see him again,' she murmured as the wind whipped her hair. 'And I shall then know if these feelings are more than just silly fantasies.'

Just then Captain MacFarlane came towards them.

"Excuse me, my Lady, Miss Preston, but as you can see, we have arrived at our destination. Would you care to go ashore or wait until his Lordship comes to join us?"

"Oh, we will wait for Papa," replied Linette. "Will you ask chef to arrange luncheon for us at midday as I am quite famished already."

"Of course, I shall tell him myself."

The Captain smiled and excused himself.

As he walked back to the bridge, Linette remarked,

"He is a very fine man, is he not? I trust him with my life."

"Yes, he is," replied Anthea, "but I would imagine that your father would engage only the best people to care for his only daughter!"

Linette laughed.

"*La Bella Napoli*!" she sighed. "It's so great to be back here. If only my time was not going to be filled with entertaining Papa's boring clients! It will be ships, ships, ships – morning, noon and night!"

"Perhaps he will allow us to sightsee. It cannot be all work for you."

"You don't know Papa. Work is everything to him. That is probably why he has never remarried."

"He has just not met the right one," replied Anthea. "When he does – "

"Not Papa," retorted Linette. "I would love to meet the woman who could drag him away from his ships!"

Chuckling to herself, Linette returned to her cabin, leaving Anthea to take in the view.

'I can see that I am going to have to do quite a lot of persuading,' she mumbled, 'and there can surely be no more romantic place on earth than Naples.'

The hours ticked slowly by and still there was no sign of the Earl. Finally, just before luncheon, a message arrived via the telegraph for Linette.

She took the message and opened it quickly.

"Oh no!" she cried, "Papa is delayed yet again. He will not be with us until tomorrow at the earliest."

"Then, we shall have to find another way to amuse ourselves," suggested Anthea her heart sinking with instant disappointment. "As we've both been so unwell, shall we send for a hairdresser to make us look beautiful?"

Linette clapped her hands together in delight.

"What a divine idea! I shall ask the hairdresser for an Italian style to impress Papa and his dull clients."

Anthea smiled as making *herself* look attractive for the Earl was precisely what she had in mind.

They sent ashore for the hairdresser who had been recommended to Linette on her last visit to Naples.

And so about an hour later, a carriage drew up and out jumped a tall elegant man named Paolo.

"Ah, *che bella*!" he declared on seeing his two new clients. "I will make you the toast of Napoli."

He sat them down in Linette's cabin and examined them both carefully.

Linette had her hair styled first with much primping by Paolo. He brushed it, trimmed it, and then curled it into an elaborate style that made Linette appear more grown up.

"*Bellissima*," he cried, surveying his handiwork.

Linette pronounced herself delighted with the result and next he turned his attention to Anthea.

He handled her lovely thick golden hair with relish and smiled seductively at her.

"Such amazing beautiful hair," he gushed. "I shall do something really special with it."

After he had finished, Anthea did not recognise the reflection that stared back from the mirror.

She looked so different, striking and more attractive and she felt certain it would have the desired effect on the Earl.

"You look wonderful," exclaimed Linette. "Now, we must go ashore and show off our new hairstyles. If we hurry, we can catch the shops. Naples is famous for coral jewellery and I would like to purchase some."

Thanking Paolo profusely, they then changed their dresses and asked the Captain to send for a carriage.

Before long they were walking around the shops in search of somewhere that sold the famous coral jewellery.

"I really wanted to treat myself to a cameo brooch, but I cannot remember where the shops are," said Linette, as Anthea, in fluent Italian, stopped a passing woman to ask where they might find such an establishment.

"Linette, this lady says that if we walk up to the end of the street and turn right, we should find one there. We shall have to leave the carriage behind as the road is too narrow."

Linette went at once to their driver and asked him to wait for them. Glad of a chance to rest, he nodded his assent and the two girls made their way up the street.

As they turned the corner as instructed, they saw a small row of shops, all selling jewellery.

"There! Look!" cried Linette, hurrying towards the first one.

She pushed open the door and a bell rang. A grey-haired man with glasses and a white moustache appeared.

Anthea had to do all the talking, as the man did not speak English.

After telling him what they wanted, he nodded and brought out a tray of the most exquisite cameo brooches.

"The workmanship is so fine," commented Anthea, holding up a coral bracelet with gold fastenings.

"I think I shall buy this brooch and earrings," said Linette decisively. "And I want you to choose something so that I can buy it for you as a gift."

"Oh, but I could not," replied Anthea, eyeing a red-coral necklace.

"I insist," responded Linette, laying her hand upon Anthea's. "If it was not for you then I would have died of boredom on the trip. No, I want you to choose something."

Anthea pointed to the necklace – it was lovely and it would be most becoming with her white linen dress.

"Would I be able to have that one?"

"Of course. You must have it to please me!"

Anthea said to the proprietor in her best Italian that they would take the necklace, the brooch and earrings, as well as another necklace for Linette.

"For such beautiful customers, I will put in extra!" he replied, winking at Anthea and slipping into her parcel a pair of red coral earrings that matched the necklace.

She thanked him and they left the shop happily.

"Where shall we go now?" asked Linette. "I don't

feel like returning to the ship just yet. And now that Papa will not be joining us until tomorrow, there is no hurry."

"Look, there is an art gallery over there," suggested Anthea, pointing across the road. "I am very fond of art and Italian painters in particular. Shall we explore?"

"Oh, yes, do let's! If I found something for Papa, he would think me very clever indeed."

They crossed the road to the gallery. It was empty save for a young assistant who sat reading in a corner. She greeted them and then returned to her book.

They examined the paintings – it seemed that two artists were exhibiting and their styles were very different.

One was a landscape artist whose canvases were of beautiful views of Naples, whilst the other artist appeared to be fond of painting young women and children.

"I do like this scene of Vesuvius," declared Linette. "Look, you can even see smoke rising from the crater."

"They are much more attractive than the portraits," whispered Anthea, as she saw a young man at the back of the gallery and did not wish to offend him if he turned out to be the artist responsible.

They stood and admired the paintings for a bit and then returned to the one Linette had first remarked upon.

"It really is quite magnificent," commented Anthea, as Linette inspected the Vesuvius painting once more.

"You like it?" came a voice behind them.

They turned to see the young man standing there.

Linette blushed.

He was around the same age as herself and very good-looking with his dark hair and deep-blue eyes.

"Yes, very much," replied Anthea.

"And you, senorina?" he addressed Linette.

She blushed furiously once more and lowered her eyes. Anthea hoped that she was not about to run off or become upset, as she had with the waiter in the restaurant in Marseilles.

"I – I think it's wonderful," she smiled at him.

"Then I am glad because it was I who painted it," he said. "If it pleases you, then I am very happy."

"You are very talented. I would love to be able to paint. My own efforts are not very remarkable."

"I am sure they are charming. But let me introduce myself. Roberto di Novelli at your service."

"I am Miss Hayworth and this is my friend Miss Preston," said Linette, casting a meaningful look at Anthea, encouraging her to join in the deception.

"Charmed," replied Roberto, taking Anthea's hand and kissing it. "Now, Miss Hayworth, would you like to see more of my work? There are several in the back room that is not open to the public."

Linette hesitated for a moment and then smiled.

"Yes, I would love to."

Anthea was surprised that she had agreed to go with Roberto, but did not make any comment.

Instead she wandered around the gallery and came across a charming painting of the Castell dell'Ovo that she assumed was also by Roberto.

'I shall buy it as a reminder of my time in Naples,' she said to herself, as she went to find the assistant.

Some thirty minutes later, Anthea had finished her business and looked around for Linette.

But there was neither sight nor sound of her. It was now getting quite late and it was obvious that the assistant was anxious to close up for the day.

Anthea asked her if she could look for Linette in the back of the gallery and the assistant led the way.

She was stunned to see Linette sitting outside in a courtyard at a table, laughing and chatting with Roberto.

Her pale skin was flushed with excitement and her deep-blue eyes were full of animation as the two talked as if there was no one else in the world.

"Linette!"

"Anthea. I am sorry – have I been here for ages? I appear to have lost all track of time."

"It is quite all right, Linette, but the assistant wishes to close up and we must be getting back to the ship."

Linette's face fell.

"Oh," she sighed, "Roberto has asked us if I – *we* would care to dine with him this evening at his house in the hills. Do say *yes*, Anthea."

Anthea regarded her eager young face and did not feel that she could refuse her, even if she felt a little uneasy at the prospect of dining out with a stranger.

"Very well," she answered eventually, "but now we should return to our carriage and then on to the ship. They will be wondering where we are."

"Of course. Roberto, will you now write down your address for us and we shall see you later this evening?"

Roberto pulled a piece of paper from his pocket and wrote down where he lived.

Handing it to Linette, she smiled and reddened.

"*Ciao*," she sighed to Roberto, as he took her hand gently and kissed it. "Until nine o'clock."

They went in search of their carriage. It was exactly where they left it with the driver asleep in his box.

Anthea coughed and he awakened with a start.

"We would like to go back to the ship now."

He took their parcels and held the door open.

"Do you like Roberto? He is very handsome, is he not?" asked Linette, almost as soon as they had sat down.

"He seems a very nice young man."

"He is very talented, don't you think? He says that he would rather paint landscapes than portraits, although he does do some. He wants to paint me by the sea at Sorrento, can you imagine?"

"Sorrento! Where is that? I don't think I can allow you to go off on your own to some strange place."

"It is only across the Bay of Naples, and you would have to come with me to chaperone me. That is, if Papa does not find something dull for me once he gets here."

The carriage sped off to the quayside where *The Sea Sprite* was docked.

Anthea did not respond to Linette's plea for her to act as chaperone while Roberto painted her. She was too shocked to see the change that had come over the girl in such a short time.

'She is so infatuated with him – I can see,' thought Anthea, as Linette prattled on about Roberto and his many virtues.

By the time they reached the ship, the Captain was anxiously pacing the deck.

"Where have you been, ladies? I was about to send out a search party for you," he grumbled, as they walked up the gangplank.

"I am sorry, but we were detained in an art gallery," replied Anthea. "I bought a painting and it all took rather longer than I expected."

The driver was unloading their parcels.

"I can see you had a pleasant time," commented the Captain. "Dinner will be at eight o'clock."

"Oh, we are not dining on board tonight," piped up Linette.

"We have been invited to a local's house – an artist we met in the gallery," put in Anthea quickly.

The Captain raised one eyebrow.

"Midshipman Jones will be most upset," he replied, with a smile at Anthea. "He was to join us."

"Then perhaps he should accompany us to dinner at Roberto's?" suggested Anthea, "and be our body guard."

"I think that would be most appropriate. I shall go at once and inform him to be ready – at what time?"

"We are expected at nine o'clock," replied Anthea. "Can the driver be ready again at half-past eight, please?"

The Captain walked off down the deck, so Anthea and Linette moved towards their cabins.

"Thank you," whispered Linette. "I thought he was about to tell me off! He is conscious that he is responsible for me and that Naples can be a rough place. Will it not be awkward with Midshipman Jones along, though, after – "

"I am certain he will do as he is told. Now, here we are, I would like a rest before we go out tonight, so I shall close the connecting door. Please wake me if you cannot hear any movement by eight o'clock."

Anthea went inside her cabin and closed the door.

She had a great deal to think about.

'I could not have foreseen this new situation with Roberto, and I can see it could lead to much trouble if not handled correctly. What will the Earl think? Whilst there is no harm in going out to dinner at Roberto's house, if Linette begins to slip out on her own to see him, it could be a problem, not to say dangerous.'

She lay down on her bed and tried to rest.

Soon she had dozed off and was woken by the gong announcing dinner.

'It must be eight. I must hurry and dress myself as the carriage will be here for us soon.'

"Hello, Anthea. I am glad you are up – I was about to get worried."

Linette had opened the connecting door and she had put on a deep sapphire dress that matched her eyes and the red coral around her throat made her skin look even whiter and set off her dark hair to perfection.

"You look so beautiful," exclaimed Anthea. "What a pity your Papa is not here to see you."

"Yes, it is a pity and I did so want him to see my new hairdo. I shall have to be very careful I do not ruin it in my sleep tonight."

"Perhaps we could request that Paolo returns to us every day and dress our hair?" suggested Anthea.

"What a wonderful idea. It will be very expensive, but it would be a great treat for us. I shall send a message to him in the morning. I hope Papa is not going to be too late tomorrow – I cannot wait to see him."

Anthea thought of the Earl as she dressed and her heart immediately began to beat faster.

'I am so looking forward to seeing him again,' she mused. 'And I really must not make him aware that I am harbouring silly fancies about him.'

"Are you ready yet?" Linette then called out.

"Almost."

"We must hurry and not keep Roberto waiting."

Anthea smiled.

'She is in love,' she thought, as she picked up her shawl. 'And for the first time. That is why she does not want to reveal that she is a lady as she fears he may think her too far above him socially.'

Their driver was waiting for them on the quayside and Midshipman Jones was already seated in the carriage and he behaved as if nothing had happened between him and Anthea, much to her relief.

Linette could hardly contain her excitement.

"I wonder what kind of house he lives in? Do you think it will be a villa?"

"I have no idea," answered Anthea, as the carriage sped towards the address Roberto had given them.

They were soon going uphill with wonderful views across Naples Bay.

Shortly the carriage stopped outside a large white-washed villa with wooden shutters.

The door opened and Roberto emerged.

"You are here," he called out. "I was worried that you would not come."

"I hope you do not mind, but Captain MacFarlane insisted on us having Midshipman Jones accompany us," explained Linette coyly.

"That is quite all right. He is a wise man as it is not always safe at night for ladies in Naples. Now do come in – we shall have aperitifs before we eat."

They walked inside and were at once struck by their surroundings.

"I did not expect anything so – "

"Grand?" responded Roberto finishing off Linette's question for her. "Yes, my Papa was a rich man."

"He is no longer with you?"

"I am afraid so – he disappeared under mysterious circumstances when I was young, but I will explain later."

He led them to a high-ceilinged room overlooking the Bay. His servant appeared and he ordered him to pour the aperitifs.

"Tell me more about your parents. Is your mother still alive?" asked Linette, as she accepted a drink.

"My Mama died a few years ago after the terrible outbreak of influenza that swept through Napoli and, as for Papa – have you ever heard of the Camorra?"

They looked blankly at Roberto.

"No," answered Linette. "Who or what is it?"

"They are an underground organisation made up of criminals who run illegal activities in Napoli. It was they who were responsible for killing my father – but they were never brought to justice."

"That is terrible. The Police did not catch them?"

Roberto laughed coldly.

"You do not 'catch' the Camorra, Miss Hayworth. They are a law unto themselves."

"But they are criminals?"

"Yes, but with some of them either in league with the Police or in their ranks themselves, it is a hopeless task. Most of the time the Police wash their hands of them."

Linette's tender heart went out to Roberto.

"He is alone," she whispered to Anthea, as he went to check on their meal. "Poor man. And he lives in terror of this Camorra."

"Linette, I am not certain that it is wise to become involved with him – "

"Hush now, he is coming back," cautioned Linette, as the door swung open and Roberto reappeared.

"If you will follow me – we shall eat now," he said, with a wide sweep of his arm.

His dining room overlooked terraced gardens with marble statues and a patio with chairs and a table.

In the middle of the room was a dining table, ready and waiting for them.

Midshipman Jones pulled back a chair for Anthea, while Roberto did likewise for Linette and then the servant filled their glasses with wine and served the first course.

"I love this soup! What is it?" quizzed Linette.

"It is *zucchini*. I am surprised that you have never had it before, as it is such a Neapolitan speciality."

"Well, if I did, then it was not as delicious as this!"

The next course was a tomato and mozzarella salad with a dish of pasta and fish sauce, while for pudding there was home-made ice cream.

After the meal they retired to the drawing room to drink cups of coffee and glasses of *limoncello* liqueur.

At midnight Midshipman Jones said that they really must return to *The Sea Sprite*.

Linette looked crestfallen and Anthea knew that she had hoped to spend some time alone with Roberto.

"So soon?" she groaned.

"Captain MacFarlane does not like any us to be out after midnight and it is not always safe to travel around the City late at night," insisted Midshipman Jones.

"Yes, supposing the Camorra were to come after us," commented Anthea.

"I would not imagine they would do that unless you were somehow in their way," joked Roberto, "for instance, if you were here to take business from under their noses."

"But Papa – "

"Ssh," cautioned Anthea.

Linette clammed up instantly but, even so, Anthea felt a shiver go down her spine.

'It is possible that the Earl knows of this gang,' she thought to herself as they bade goodbye to Roberto. 'And he knows how dangerous it is for Linette to be out alone in Naples. If this Camorra is trying to gain a foothold in the shipping business, then she could be at risk.'

As the carriage pulled away, Roberto slipped a note into Linette's hand and she held onto it until they arrived back at the ship and then, as soon as Midshipman Jones had left them, she took it out and read it eagerly.

"He wants me to go for a drive with him tomorrow afternoon!"

"You won't be able to," answered Anthea calmly. "Your father will be here."

"Nonsense! As soon as he does arrive, he will be ensconced with a load of boring businessmen talking about ships. If he wants someone attractive to go with him and charm them into placing orders, then you should go in my place – and what is more, I shall suggest it!"

"I am not certain – "

"Oh, Anthea, please promise me you will let me go out with Roberto. You could tell Papa that I was having a gown fitted or find some other excuse."

"But I am supposed to be with you at all times – "

"We will think of a way around that. And you must promise me, too, that you will not breathe a word to Papa about Roberto. At least not just yet."

Anthea's mind was in a whirl.

What she was asking of her was not only deceitful but could have repercussions. What if anything happened to her? And after the Earl had placed his trust in her?

Anthea also could not imagine how Linette would be able to slip past Captain MacFarlane, as he had already proved himself to be very efficient at looking out for her.

Yet she could not deny that the chance of spending a great deal of time with the handsome Earl, whom she had been thinking about constantly during the past week, was a highly attractive one that filled her with eager anticipation.

'Could I possibly lie to the Earl?' she asked herself, as Linette continued to plead with her. 'After all, it would mean having him to myself for a while – '

"I shall think about it, Linette. Now go to bed."

'Would it be wrong to help her?' thought Anthea, as she got ready to retire. 'Or am I just wanting to help her to for my own ends?'

This conundrum was keeping her awake long after five bells had sounded in the clear night air.

CHAPTER SEVEN

Although she had hardly slept Anthea rose early the next morning. Wrapping herself in her dressing gown, she crept out on to the deck to view the scene.

The sun was already warm and it was to be another fine day, even though it was almost October.

'I wonder if the Earl has docked yet?' she said to herself, as she scanned the private yachts and steamships berthed in the harbour. 'How I long to see him!'

Her thoughts returned to the subject of Linette and the deception she had asked her to engage in.

'Although I have every sympathy with her situation – she is young and in love – I must not allow myself to be swayed from what I think is right. The Earl has charged me with being her chaperone and I must do so rigorously.'

She wondered just how she would break the news to Linette and sighed heavily.

'It will not be pleasant informing her that I will not lie for her.'

At breakfast she broke the news to Linette.

A sulky pout appeared on her face, even though she said she understood.

"Of course, Papa would be furious if he found out that you were lying for me – I understand completely."

"So you will not go with Roberto this afternoon?"

Linette paused,

"*We shall see.*"

Fear clutched at Anthea's heart.

She was now seeing a new side of Linette, a steely resolve she could only have inherited from her father.

Beneath the girlish exterior was a wilful character, bent on getting whatever she desired.

They finished breakfast in silence.

Anthea felt grateful when Midshipman Jones came to inform them that the Earl's ship had docked and he had sent word that he would board *The Sea Sprite* shortly.

"I don't expect you to lie for me, but do promise me you will not say a word to Papa about Roberto," asked Linette, as they rose to leave. "I will tell him in my own time and if I can persuade Papa to allow you to go to his meetings in my stead, will you agree?"

"Very well. Now shall we sit up on deck until your father does arrive? It would be a shame to be stuck in our cabins on such a lovely day."

Anthea felt that the atmosphere between the two of them was a bit strained as Jackson set out their deck chairs.

They both read in silence for most of the morning, only commenting about a passing seabird or the weather.

At last just after midday, there was a commotion on deck that heralded the arrival of the Earl.

He came striding towards them his arms open.

"Papa!" cried Linette, leaping up.

"Linette, my darling. I am so sorry I was delayed. It was a few days before I could placate Prince Aristos and assure him that his ship would be just as he wanted it."

"And he is happy now, Papa?"

"Very much so. You look well and somehow more grown up. How could that be in so short a time?"

Linette preened herself delightedly.

"I have had my hair restyled in the Italian manner," she answered. "And I have also been out shopping – "

"I am so glad that you have found ways to amuse yourself and indeed I have to thank you, Miss Preston, for accompanying her. I slept much more easily knowing that she was in not one, but two pairs of safe hands – yours and Captain MacFarlane's!"

Anthea blushed as his piercing amber eyes regarded her warmly. She felt overcome with so many emotions.

The Earl was every bit as handsome as she recalled and the longing she felt to be in his presence intensified.

"Now Jackson is here with coffee and I want you to tell me everything you have seen and done so far. This is your first time in Naples, Miss Preston?"

"Yes, it is."

"And has it lived up to your expectations?"

"Even more so," she replied, feeling oddly tongue-tied. She blushed again and looked down into her coffee, not knowing what to say next.

Just then Jackson came in again to inform them that luncheon would be served in half an hour's time.

"Excellent," exclaimed the Earl. "I hope that chef is preparing some Neapolitan specialities for us. I always ask him to cook local dishes wherever we happen to be."

Linette dominated the conversation and Anthea was happy to keep quiet.

Even so she felt the Earl's eyes on her constantly and she could not meet them without reddening.

Just before luncheon was served, Linette excused herself and left them alone.

Anthea, although delighted, felt a little awkward.

"I have to thank you for taking such good care of my daughter," the Earl said, moving closer to her. "She is the most precious thing in the world to me and I would die if any harm came to her."

"She is very easy to look after. And so delightful."

"Even so, I want you to know how grateful I am – I shall, of course, be remunerating you and have made funds available to Captain MacFarlane to distribute when he pays the ship's company."

"Oh, it's not necessary, as I have my own money."

She was secretly relieved, as, in her sudden flight, she had only been able to take a little cash with her.

The Earl laid his hand on hers as it rested on the arm of her steamer chair.

"Thank you again," he murmured and looked deep into her eyes.

Her heart leapt into her mouth as his hand remained there for a second longer, and she felt a surge of affection – so much so, that she was forced to look away.

There was an uneasy silence as the Earl retracted his hand and sat back in his chair. The world seemed to be spinning faster as Anthea tried to compose herself.

"Luncheon is served, my Lord," intoned Jackson.

"Thank you, Jackson," replied the Earl, getting up. "Miss Preston, shall we go to the Saloon? I wonder where Linette is? She has been gone for a while now."

They sat down at the table and fifteen minutes later, Linette appeared looking as white a sheet.

"Goodness, you do look pale!" called Anthea. "Are you feeling unwell?"

"Yes," murmured Linette. "I have been sick and I fear that I have a migraine coming on."

"That is a pity, my darling. Chef has prepared your favourite lobster salad and who will come with me now to this important meeting after luncheon? My clients were so looking forward to meeting you."

Linette turned towards Anthea.

"Why, you can take Miss Preston here. She speaks fluent Italian and I am certain that she will charm them as much, if not more so, than I could."

Anthea scrutinised Linette's wan face.

As her eyes swept over her, she noticed specks of talcum powder around her hairline.

'The little minx!' she then thought. 'She has faked this migraine so that she can slip away and see Roberto!'

Anthea did not say a word as she knew that if she exposed Linette's deception she would not have the chance to spend time alone with the Earl.

'While we would not be on our own for most of the time, at least we will have the journey there and back,' she lectured herself. 'I reckon I should expose Linette, but I do not think I have the heart to do so.'

And so she did not say a word when, after a few mouthfuls, Linette pronounced that she was too ill to eat and excused herself to return to her cabin.

"Well, Miss Preston, it appears it has been left to *you* to help save the day," commented the Earl.

"Before we leave, I feel I should inform you about the people we are going to see. It is vital that you should impress them, as we are in competition with the Germans and it is imperative that we win this order."

"I will certainly do my very best, my Lord."

"Excellent. Usually Linette so entrances everyone with her beauty that they forget themselves and the orders are easily extracted. You are every bit as beautiful as my daughter and I beg of you, please don't let me down!"

Anthea felt herself swelling with pride.

'He thinks that I am beautiful,' she said to herself happily. 'And he is very attentive, but I must be careful as there are many men who are charming to every female they come across and make them fall in love with them, when really they have no romantic intentions at all. Did Linette not say that many women had set their cap at him, only to be disappointed?'

"Miss Preston?"

He was regarding her with a quizzical expression.

"Oh, I am sorry, I was so very deep in thought."

"I was saying that we should leave very soon. My meeting with the Benedettis is at two-thirty."

"I will go my cabin and fetch my parasol and hat."

"Then I shall see you in ten minutes."

The reflection in the mirror inside her cabin showed that Anthea's face was burning as she put on her hat.

'I must try to calm myself,' she told her reflection. 'I must not appear unduly flustered to the Earl.'

She took a last look at herself, and then, picking up her parasol, she left her cabin.

She hesitated for a moment outside Linette's cabin, wondering whether she should caution her not to leave the ship without an escort, but instead she went on her way.

The Earl stood waiting on deck and she could see a fine open carriage was already sitting on the quayside.

She walked towards it beside him feeling her heart knocking hard against her ribs.

Soon they were on their way to the heart of Naples, being pulled by a team of handsome white horses.

"How do you find Naples in comparison with other Italian cities?" asked the Earl, as they trotted along.

"It is enchanting, but I have so far not seen enough of the City to satisfy me."

"It would take many weeks to see everything that Naples has to offer. I have been coming here for years and still find new things to delight and impress."

"A local told us about the Camorra," said Anthea, bravely introducing the topic. "Have you ever come across them? They really do sound frightening."

The Earl's face darkened.

"Yes, I have," he replied curtly. "And all who do business in Naples are wary of treading on their toes."

"So they have not tried to inveigle themselves into your particular business, my Lord?"

"They have attempted to do so in the past, but they have to contend with the fact that Italian ships are greatly inferior to British or even German-built vessels."

"So they could still interfere with your business?"

"It's a remote possibility, Miss Preston, but do not concern yourself with the actions of criminals. My clients are strong enough to stand up to them."

Anthea felt a little reassured.

'Perhaps Roberto was over-emphasising the danger they present,' she thought. 'He would not inform us if the reason his father had come to a sticky end was because of shady dealings of any kind. As we were perfect strangers to him, why should he?'

At last the carriage came to a halt outside an ornate building in the business district of town.

"Here we are," said the Earl as the driver got down to open the carriage door for them. "We are right on time, although we must expect our hosts to be a little delayed – that is the way of things in Naples."

True to his word, they were kept waiting until his clients had returned from their luncheon.

"Everyone eats much later in Naples than we do at home," explained the Earl. "It is not unusual for people not to dine until eleven o'clock at night for instance!"

"I don't think I could wait that long," commented Anthea. "I much prefer to eat early."

"Very wise. Oh, look, here is Signor Benedetti."

A short middle-aged man in a suit came towards the Earl and greeted him in a stream of Italian. He seemed very pleased to see him.

"And this is Miss Preston, my assistant," said the Earl, introducing her. "She also speaks Italian, so there is no need for you to bring in an interpreter for her."

Signor Benedetti seized Anthea's hand and kissed it, pronouncing her charming.

He then led them upstairs to a large room in which sat a number of elderly gentlemen.

Anthea was seated next to one of the younger men, who paid her a great deal of attention.

'Linette was not exaggerating,' she said to herself, as the assembled men droned on and on about certain ship-building technicalities. 'If it were not for Signor Martinelli next to me, I would have difficulty in keeping awake!'

At last after several hours spent wrangling over the details of the order, Signor Benedetti stood up and shook the Earl by the hand.

"Then, we have a deal," he announced in English.

Anthea was delighted.

The Earl smiled warmly at her as they all rose from the table to shake his hand.

Later when they were once again in their carriage, the Earl thanked her profusely.

"I expect you heard all Signor Benedetti said – that you are as beautiful as you are intelligent. He was most impressed with your Italian and your contribution helped enormously winning me the contract."

"Nonsense, my Lord, I did nothing more than smile sweetly and talk to Signor Martinelli next to me."

"You were *my lucky star*!" replied the Earl. "And tomorrow I shall be signing the contract. I had expected our negotiations to take a good deal longer, but everything went so smoothly, I can only attribute it to your presence!

"Now, we must hurry back to the ship – I am most anxious to see how Linette is. I have never known her to suffer a migraine before and hope this is not an unfortunate omen for the future."

'I shall have to have a word with Linette,' Anthea told herself. 'She should not deceive her father and break his trust. Oh, I do so wish she had not put me in such an uncomfortable position.'

But on returning to *The Sea Sprite*, they could not find Linette anywhere.

Eventually the Earl asked one of the crew.

"She went ashore hours ago, my Lord."

"What, on her own?"

"I am sorry, my Lord – I don't know, everyone else has gone ashore. As I myself did not see her Ladyship, I could not say whether or not she was unaccompanied."

"I am sure that someone would have gone with her, perhaps Midshipman Jones," soothed Anthea, knowing full well that it was highly likely that Linette had slipped off on her own. "He comes with us whenever we go out."

"I would hope so. I have often told her it is unsafe for foreigners to go wandering around Naples. There have been kidnappings of strangers – "

His voice trailed off and Anthea wanted to reassure him, but she knew she would be a hypocrite if she did.

"Would you care to join me for coffee?" asked the Earl suddenly. "If I do not have company, I will only sit and worry about Linette until she returns."

"If I am not distracting you from more important matters, I would love to," replied Anthea delighted.

"I don't think I could concentrate on anything until I know that Linette is safe. Come, we will see if Jackson is still on board."

The Earl rang and Jackson appeared.

"Jackson, we should like some coffee and tell me, did Lady Linette go ashore alone this afternoon?"

Jackson hesitated and glanced over at Anthea.

"I was not here when she left the ship, my Lord, so I am afraid I could not say."

'She has gone on her own!' thought Anthea.

She sensed Jackson was uneasy even if the Earl had not picked up on it.

As Jackson left the room, the Earl turned to Anthea.

"So, Miss Preston – I have not had the opportunity to discover more about you and how you met Linette."

Anthea thought quickly – she knew that if she told him she had run away from an arranged marriage, the Earl might not be impressed.

"We met in Monsieur Henri's establishment just off Bond Street. I went there to buy a new gown and Linette was in the next cubicle. I could not help overhearing her commenting upon the fact that she was about to travel to Italy and had no chaperone and so I came to the rescue!"

"That was most generous of you. Were your parents quite happy for you to go off with a stranger like that?"

"Oh, my father knows of you by reputation – he is Sir Edward Preston of Mount Street. I believe you have a house in nearby Park Lane?"

"Yes indeed, but I'm afraid, as Linette has probably told you, I am not one for socialising on the London scene. Business has kept me so busy and I prefer the quiet life. I spend a great deal of time at our house in Surrey."

"Yes, Linette did tell me."

"And you mentioned that you had a stepmother, so what has happened to Lady Preston?"

Anthea hung her head and tried not to cry.

"She is dead, my Lord," she answered him quietly.

"Oh, I am so sorry. I did not realise – "

"It was earlier in the year – and very suddenly. An illness. I was abroad at the time and had to come back to England. Papa has since remarried."

The Earl regarded her for a long moment and then slowly nodded his head.

"And do I take it you that don't get on too well with your stepmother?"

Anthea blushed furiously.

"I am sorry if I have given you an unfavourable impression, my Lord – "

The Earl laughed and shook his head.

"No, it's not what you have said, but what you have not said. It explains your eagerness to drop everything in London and accompany Linette to Italy."

"It was sheer serendipity and I did not wish to live as my stepmother dictated. Papa – "

Her voice trailed off.

101

"He is a different man since he remarried, then?"

Anthea nodded.

There was a silence as they drank their coffee. She could see that the Earl was thinking hard.

"Miss Preston," he began tentatively. "There is one question I would ask you – but it is a very personal one."

"Please, continue, my Lord."

"You will please forgive me commenting upon the fact that you are a little older than Linette, but it does rather beg the question why you are not married with a husband of your own?"

Anthea set down her cup.

"It – is – a somewhat sad tale," she stammered. "I was once engaged to someone, but he – he jilted me."

"Oh, I am sorry," replied the Earl with a concerned look. "I trust that my asking you such a question has not caused you any pain? It must have been dreadful for you. I did not mean to pry, but, as you can understand, I only wish to discover more about you."

"It is quite all right, my Lord. You are perfectly at liberty to ask whatever you so wish. You are entrusting me with the care of your daughter and it is only right that you enquire as to my character.

"Linette is such an impulsive girl and engaged me without your knowledge and I certainly expected that you might wish to know more about me."

"You must not think that I am interviewing you. I trust Linette, even if she can be a little headstrong at times, and Captain MacFarlane speaks well of you, so they cannot both be wrong. It's not always been easy for me, as Linette craves a mother figure since her own mother died."

'Here is my chance!' she decided, as she screwed up her courage to ask the Earl her burning question.

"You have not remarried?" she asked him gingerly.

"No," he replied without a hint of embarrassment. "I know some men require a wife as an absolute necessity, but Linette and I have managed perfectly well on our own. And with my business occupying so much of my time – "

His eyes took on a faraway look as he paused mid-sentence. Anthea wondered what or of whom he thought.

'Perhaps there has been a love that Linette does not know about,' she mused with an unknown fear clutching at her heart. 'Or perhaps there is still a sweetheart – '

Just then, the door to the Saloon burst open and in walked Linette, looking as if she was touching the stars.

"Jackson said I would find you in here," she called casually. "I am sorry I was not here when you returned. I felt better and wanted some air, so I went out for a drive with Midshipman Jones."

Anthea stared at her crossly.

'She does not even seek to keep up the pretence of having been ill!' she said to herself. 'Surely her father can see that she is right as rain?'

"You are a naughty girl," he chided fondly. "But if you had a member of the crew with you, then I am happy you are now feeling better. Did the ship's doctor give you something?"

Linette paused.

'It's so obvious that she's lying, why can he not see it?' fumed Anthea inwardly.

But the indulgent Earl was obviously wrapped right around Linette's delicate little finger.

"Yes," she answered her father eventually in a tone that told Anthea she was indeed lying.

"I am glad you are feeling better, dearest," he said, moving over to kiss the top of her head. "Shall I ring for tea? You don't want your migraine to return and I have heard that coffee is not good for headaches."

Linette smiled indulgently and the Earl sprang up to ring for Jackson.

Anthea meanwhile was feeling angry.

'He was just about to tell me something significant, when she comes wafting in as if nothing had happened! I am sure she was with Roberto – why else would she look as if she had just been given the sun, moon and stars?'

"Did your meeting go well, Papa?" asked Linette, throwing herself down in a chair.

"Yes, very – thanks to Miss Preston here, but there is another matter I wish to discuss with you – in private. Miss Preston, I hope you will not be offended if I ask you leave us alone for a while?"

'He has twigged that she is lying,' thought Anthea, before replying that she did not mind in the least.

She closed the door of the Saloon and wondered if she should seek out Midshipman Jones.

'I may well be doing Linette a disservice and, even though she did see Roberto, she may have asked him to accompany her.'

But Midshipman Jones was nowhere to be found.

She returned to her cabin and sat there fretting.

'If the Earl worms it out of Linette that she was not ill, then he may reconsider my position as her chaperone as he will guess that I knew too,' she thought glumly. 'To not have him trust me or worse to send me packing back home would be a disaster.'

Wringing her hands Anthea tried to occupy herself until Linette returned to her cabin.

'Have I now lost the Earl's trust?' she muttered, as she paced up and down. 'Oh, I could not bear it if I have.'

CHAPTER EIGHT

Next morning Linette breezed into Anthea's cabin, oblivious to the consternation she had caused the previous afternoon.

"Oh, please don't be cross with me!" cried Linette, as Anthea told her off for being so reckless. "Roberto and I had a wonderful time, do you not want to hear about it?"

"You don't seem to understand, Linette. If you had not persuaded your father that Midshipman Jones had, in fact, accompanied you, then he would have been very cross with both of us if he had discovered the truth."

"It was not a complete lie," pouted Linette, twisting her gloves in her hand. "Midshipman Jones came as far as Roberto's house and then left us. And after I left Roberto's house, the driver was with me. So, you can see – I was not totally alone."

"I fear you don't understand the situation, Linette," warned Anthea. "Don't you realise that as your Papa holds me responsible, should anything happen to you, then I shall be shipped straight back to England?"

"Oh, I had not thought of that," said Linette, a little sulkily. "I am sorry – I have no wish to get you into hot water, but it is just that I love Roberto so! Now, I want to tell you all about yesterday afternoon. It was *heavenly*!"

She chattered on and Anthea was forced to listen.

"He has already asked me to marry him!"

Anthea sat bolt upright and asked her to repeat what she had just said.

"I hope you have *not* said 'yes', Linette."

"We want to run away together and marry – Papa will have a purple fit as I am not yet twenty-one, but here in Italy, people are not so strict."

Anthea got up from her chair with her eyes blazing.

She was trying to control her anger, but was finding it very difficult in the face of Linette's irresponsibility.

"You must think this through carefully. And how will you live? Roberto is a struggling artist and the money his parents left him will not last for ever."

"He has heaps of money! And I have an income – "

"Which your Papa will stop if you displease him in this way. Linette, I beg you, think of what you are doing."

"Well, if you feel like that – " she answered, getting up and slamming shut the connecting doors to their cabins.

'Really,' muttered Anthea under her breath. 'They say that love makes one bold, but Linette takes it too far.'

She was interrupted by a knock on her cabin door. Thinking that it might be Midshipman Jones coming to see what they wished to do that day, she went to open it.

Instead of Midshipman Jones, it was the Earl!

"Oh, my Lord, I was not expecting you."

"I am sorry, but there is to be a further meeting at Benedetti's and I was hoping you would accompany me. It is my fault for not mentioning it last night at dinner. But Linette did not give me the opportunity to say anything as she so dominated the conversation!"

"I would be delighted to come with you, my Lord, I do hope that nothing is untoward?"

"Not at all. It is just that I am sure the Benedettis would be delighted to see you again. They are taking us for a grand luncheon and I would like you to come as my guest, by way of my saying 'thank you'."

"But I have done nothing. It is all your doing – you are so brilliant that I am certain you would have still left with the contract without my being there."

"Nevertheless, I wish you to be my guest."

"And Linette?"

"She has promised me – no more gallivanting. I have arranged for one of the crew to take her to luncheon and, then, an art gallery. I do not wish to alarm you, but I have been told that the Camorra are highly displeased that I have won this order. As a result it is imperative that neither of you goes around alone."

"I thought they did not present a problem to you?"

"That was until I secured the Benedetti order. They have some involvement in the shipyards here and I would not put it past them to try and ruin my negotiations. Now as I have some work to do, can you meet me in an hour?"

'Linette will not like this at all,' thought Anthea as the Earl left. 'I would wager that she will do all she can to slip away and meet Roberto. I should go and warn her not to leave the ship without a chaperone of some description.'

She went to the door, but all was quiet.

'Perhaps she's asleep,' thought Anthea, pushing the door open a little.

But Linette was not in her cabin.

'She has slipped out again! The little fool!'

Running out of the cabin and along the gangway, Anthea bumped straight into Midshipman Jones.

"Have you seen Lady Linette?" he enquired looking flustered. "His Lordship has now ordered me to take her out sightseeing today, but she is nowhere to be found."

"No, I was coming to ask you the very same thing. I do believe she has given both of us the slip."

"His Lordship will be furious. What shall we do?"

"If I tell you where she is, promise that you will go and find her, but you must not tell his Lordship?"

"Anything, as long as she is safe."

"Here, this is the address of where I believe her to be. Go there and tell her that you have been instructed not to leave her side. Tell her that the Camorra is up in arms at her father's latest deal and she will understand. If not, then the person she is with will insist she obeys you."

Midshipman Jones looked at her in awe.

"It is the address of Roberto di Novelli! You are so clever, as well as beautiful," he said, permitting himself the luxury of a fond look. "If you had not been here, I dread to think what might have happened."

"There is no need to tell his Lordship. Now, go. I will say that I have seen you both leave. His Lordship is occupied in his cabin and will not know any different."

Midshipman Jones hurried to a waiting carriage.

Anthea sighed with exasperation.

'Linette really is the limit!' she muttered to herself. 'Now, I must go and get ready for this luncheon.'

Her heart was now beating faster and faster – and not just with excitement.

She knew that if the Camorra had the Earl as their target, then being with him could lead to danger.

'But as long as I am with him, I will not worry,' she sighed, putting on her hat.

*

As Anthea and the Earl drove to their appointment, she could not help but constantly be on her guard.

Her eyes scanned the crowds in the bustling streets, searching for signs of anything out of the ordinary.

'I have no idea what the Camorra might look like,' 'but if I am alert, then I can be ready should anyone mount an attack on us.'

"You don't seem very relaxed today," remarked the Earl as they drove along. "I do hope that what I said about the Camorra has not frightened you."

"I must confess that I am a little unnerved."

"Then you must not be. You are safe with me."

The Earl moved a little closer to her and smiled.

She felt her heart leap as she looked into his amber eyes. The sun was shining and she could almost imagine herself drowning in their silky depths.

'I must control myself,' she thought, as the carriage reached its destination. 'Did not Mama say that I always showed on my face whatever I was feeling? I do not want him thinking I am a love-struck ninny!'

The Earl then helped her from the carriage and they walked towards the restaurant.

As they did so, Anthea could have sworn that she could see someone spying on them from the shadows, but when she looked again, there was no one there.

"Are you all right?" the Earl asked her.

"It is nothing. I am just anxious to make an equally good impression on the Benedettis as last time."

"Of course you will and they will be charmed and entranced by you again. Now come, let us proceed."

He offered her his arm and she tucked hers beneath it. Standing so close to him, she could feel his warmth and she longed to stay like that forever.

"Lord Hayworth!" Signor Benedetti, rising from the table, shook the Earl's hand. "And *La Bella* Miss Preston – you honour us again with your beauty."

The Earl smiled at Anthea as if to reassure her that all was well as they sat down.

"Here's to our new fleet of ships," toasted Signor Benedetti, raising his glass and the table followed suit.

Anthea was glowing with pride as she put her glass to her lips and the Earl was looking at her and smiling.

Her heart leapt and she felt herself blushing.

'Could I dare to hope he has feelings for me?' she mused, as they chatted in Italian. 'I would give anything if I thought he cared.'

*

Meanwhile up on the hill at Roberto's, Linette was rather grumpily opening the door to Midshipman Jones.

"I am sorry, my Lady, but Miss Preston was most insistent that I come and find you. His Lordship thinks we are out for a drive in any case."

"I am not a child," sulked Linette. "Papa is being just beastly."

Midshipman Jones coloured and immediately she felt bad for taking out her ill humour on him.

"You had better come in," she sighed. "Roberto and I are just beginning luncheon, but I am certain that he can stretch to another guest."

He took off his cap before following her inside.

"Midshipman Jones," called out Roberto, "will you not sit down and eat with us? There is plenty."

"Papa has sent him after me. I am sorry, Roberto, it is such a bore."

"It was not him, my Lady – it was Miss Preston who asked me to come. She has sworn me not to tell your father that you are here and, as long as you stay put, I will not say anything to him. I shall tell him that I brought you here and was with you all the time."

Linette eyed him cautiously,

"Very well. Roberto and I were intending to visit a Church this afternoon and you can come with us, but only if you promise to stay in the carriage while we are inside."

"I am not certain – "

"Oh, don't be stuffy, Jones! I promise faithfully I will not give you the slip again. You have been very kind not telling Papa where I was and I appreciate that."

"Very well, my Lady, but I shall be watching you very carefully from now on!"

*

The luncheon with the Benedettis was progressing smoothly. After the main course, Signor Benedetti brought out a contract and everyone signed it.

The Earl paused as he dipped his quill in the ink.

"This is a great moment for me, Signor Benedetti," he murmured with a quaver in his voice.

Anthea could tell that he was quite overcome.

'But perhaps I do not realise the significance of this deal,' she pondered. 'Did not Signor Benedetti mention a fleet of ships? I was rather under the impression that it was only one ship he was hoping to build.'

The Earl signed the document with a grand flourish and the whole table broke into spontaneous applause.

To Anthea's surprise he then blushed deeply as he accepted their compliments.

"To the finest fleet of ships in the whole of Italy!" he exclaimed raising his glass.

After which the Benedettis proposed another toast,

"To the beautiful Miss Preston!"

And it was now Anthea's turn to blush as she shyly raised her glass along with the others at the table.

"I would most honoured if you would agree to dine with me tonight," whispered Signor Martinelli into her ear.

Anthea smiled in reply and did not say a word.

Much as she would find it a pleasant diversion, she had eyes only for the Earl and did not wish to lead on the handsome Signor Martinelli.

At last the luncheon drew to a close and Anthea was shocked to hear a Church bell chime four o'clock as they climbed back into their waiting carriage.

"Goodness! Is it really that late?" she muttered, as the carriage pulled away from the kerb.

"The Italians love doing business over a luncheon and they do not like to be rushed," replied the Earl with a smile. "I hope you enjoyed it, Miss Preston?"

"Oh, immensely. Even if I now feel a bit unsteady from so much champagne! I shall need to retire for a nap before dinner."

"I do hope that Linette has not been too bored in the company of Midshipman Jones," said the Earl. "Although he is of her own age, he is very quiet and Linette is fond of colourful characters."

Anthea fell silent.

She hoped that Midshipman Jones had managed to catch up with her at Roberto's house and that they had not already gone out somewhere by the time he arrived.

'If the Earl's business with the Benedettis has now finished, the three of us can do things together before we leave Naples,' she mused. 'Linette would not dare to run off to see Roberto if her father was with us all the time.'

Just then, the Earl spoke up, interrupting her train of thought.

"I do hope you were not offended that I asked you such a personal question yesterday when we were alone."

"No, not at all, my Lord."

"It is just that I find it rather hard to comprehend why such a beautiful woman as you is without a husband. However, having told me the reason, I can understand why you could be reluctant to be involved romantically again –"

Anthea looked into his eyes and was lost for words.

They held each other's gaze before the Earl looked away.

'He does care! I know he does,' she thought. 'But is it that he believes me to be uninterested in romance that prevents him declaring himself or is there another reason? I sense there is more to this mystery than meets the eye.'

"It is true that I was very upset by what happened to me," she answered slowly. "But that was six years ago and I am still young enough to make someone a good wife."

"I would not dispute that and I believe that Signor Martinelli is very much of the same mind!"

Anthea was horrified.

'Does he think I am interested in Signor Martinelli? That will not do at all.'

"He is very kind, but there is no point in embarking on a romance with someone who does not live in England."

But the Earl's attention was distracted as she spoke by their driver shouting at a slow pony and cart that had pulled out in front of them.

The Earl took out his watch impatiently.

"I was hoping to spend time with Linette before dinner," he said without responding to her pointed remark.

'Perhaps I am just mistaken after all,' she thought, miserably. 'And I am just raising my hopes for no reason. He is just being polite in taking an interest in me. I should not read too much into it.'

By the time they returned to *The Sea Sprite* she had convinced herself that her earlier impression was incorrect, and that the Earl was not interested in her in the least.

"Papa!"

Anthea heaved a sigh of relief to see Linette waving at them as their carriage drew up alongside the ship.

"Darling. Have you had an enjoyable afternoon?"

"Yes, I did, Papa. But enough of my day, I want to hear all about your deal. Did you and Signor Benedetti sign the contract?"

"Yes, we did, and what is more, he has ordered not one – but a whole fleet of ships. There will be some very disgruntled Italians and Germans in Naples this day!"

"You are so brilliant, Papa," cooed Linette, "to steal the order out from under their noses like that, now come to the Saloon and tell me all about it."

Anthea stood on the quay momentarily forgotten as father and daughter walked laughing towards the Saloon.

She quickly followed them up the gangplank and then decided to go to her cabin for a rest.

'I can see that I am guilty of misreading the Earl's intentions,' she murmured, as she tearfully closed her cabin door. 'I don't wish to come away with a broken heart, so the sooner I pull myself together, the better.'

Just before dinner, Linette opened the connecting door between their cabins.

"You are angry with me," she asked looking upset.

"Yes, Linette. "I do not care for the way you are behaving at all. I know that you are in love, but that does not mean that you can disregard the rest of us."

Linette looked taken aback, it was the first time that Anthea had spoken in such harsh terms to her and it was a shock to her.

"You don't want me to be happy?"

"It is not that – it's a matter of being sensible. How many times do we have to warn you about the danger here? Your father winning this important contract has meant that he is treading on the toes of the Camorra and Roberto can tell you how ill-advised that can be – "

"Oh, nonsense! Just because they killed Roberto's father does not mean that they are after mine! They almost never go after foreigners or so Roberto says."

Anthea's eyes were blazing as she replied,

"And your Roberto is so clever and wonderful that if these men came after you to harm you, he would shield you, would he?"

Linette suddenly looked dubious.

Roberto may be handsome, but he was accustomed to using his hands to paint rather fight or wield weapons. Even Linette could see that he was not strong enough to protect her and, what was more, he lived alone.

"He has asked me to go out for a drive with him tomorrow – what am I to tell him? He is expecting me."

Anthea got up and walked over to Linette with such a stern look upon her face that she almost shrank from her.

"Never mind tomorrow. I don't wish to spoil your fun, but we have to take what your father says seriously. If he does not need me to attend a meeting, I am coming with you whether you like it or not!"

Anthea could see that Linette was close to tears.

There was a tense minute when she felt that Linette might flee, but instead she nodded her head in agreement.

"Very well, Anthea. You are right, of course, and I am being a perfect fool. But I love Roberto so and want to make the most of every second I am in Naples – you must understand that?"

"I do," replied Anthea, softly, thinking of the Earl. "But that does not excuse thoughtless behaviour."

"Will I see you at dinner?" stammered Linette.

"Yes," answered Anthea shortly.

"And you will not tell Papa about Roberto?"

"Only if you promise to tell him yourself and that is *final*."

Linette's face was full of misery.

She knew that if she owned up, then the likelihood was that her father might prevent her from seeing Roberto.

As she closed the door behind her, Anthea heaved a sigh. It had upset her to have to speak to Linette not once, but twice, in such a fashion, but the girl did not seem to be paying any heed to her.

'If the Earl discovers our deception, he will almost certainly send both of us home at once,' she thought. 'Even if Linette tells him about Roberto now, it could still make him very angry – not just with her, but with me.

'And where will that leave me and where will I go? I just cannot return to London and an arranged marriage – I would rather weather the wrath of the Earl than that.'

She was still ruminating about her dilemma as she made her way to the Saloon later that evening.

'I do hope that by now Linette has told her father everything,' she said to herself. 'I must steel myself to be sent back home, but, if necessary, I shall throw myself on his mercy!

'Oh, Mama, hear me in Heaven, please help me!'

CHAPTER NINE

Anthea took several deep breaths before she entered the Saloon and was a little disappointed to find Linette and the Earl laughing and joking as if nothing had happened.

'She has not yet told him,' she thought, as the Earl welcomed her.

She cast a look at Linette, who was gazing down at her shoes with a guilty expression on her face.

'Perhaps I shall leave them alone after the meal and she will tell him then,' she reflected, accepting the aperitif the Earl was offering her.

After dinner Anthea rose and made her excuses. As she left the Saloon, she gave Linette a meaningful look and hoped that she would take the hint.

But at breakfast the next morning Linette confessed that she had not had the courage to tell her father about Roberto.

"We were having such fun and it did not seem right to suddenly introduce a subject that could make everything unpleasant," she explained, refusing to meet Anthea's eyes.

"I cannot pretend I am not disappointed, Linette, but I can understand why you would not wish to spoil an evening alone with your father. You must promise me that you will tell him all at the very first opportunity, but, in the meantime, what are the arrangements you have made with Roberto for today?"

"He wants me to sit for him in his garden. We had

planned on eating luncheon at his house and, then, Roberto will want to continue painting me."

"In that case, I will come with you to his house and then go for a ride. You must promise me faithfully that you will not set foot outside the door. Do you agree?"

"Yes, Anthea. Papa did warn me last night about these Camorra people and I can see now that you were not exaggerating. I promise you, I will be more careful."

"Good, I do not wish to curtail your fun or for us to fall out. I hope you understand the situation is serious."

"I do. And I know that Roberto just did not wish to frighten me when he said I should not worry about them. Papa is such an important man that I do not think Roberto realises how vulnerable that makes him."

"Good, now get ready and we shall leave presently. I wish to call in and see your father before we go – is he in his cabin?"

"I would imagine so. Even though he has no more meetings, he is working very hard on the final design of the Benedetti ships. He wants them to show to Italy, if not the world, how brilliant he is."

Anthea set down her napkin and left the table.

It was an overcast day and she could see that storm clouds were gathering over Vesuvius and she wondered if she should take an umbrella.

The air felt quite heavy and almost before she had reached the Earl's cabin, she was feeling hot and sticky.

"Come in!"

The Earl's rich voice summoned her and she felt her stomach flip as she saw him there, seated at his desk.

"Good day, Miss Preston. What brings you here?"

"I wanted to see if you have any appointments that you would wish me to attend today?"

"No, your work here is done for the time being," he smiled. "You must go out and enjoy yourself with Linette, as I fear the weather may break and you'll be soaked to the skin."

"That would be a great pity as I had hoped to see Pompeii before we sailed away and I am assuming that our departure is fairly imminent, now that your business is all but concluded."

The Earl laughed.

"There is still much work for me to do before that can happen, so I do hope you will not mind if we remain in Naples a little while longer. Once the designs have been approved, then we shall return to England."

"Thank you, my Lord," she said, turning to leave.

"Oh, Miss Preston – one other matter. I don't wish to alarm you, but I would remind you once again about the threat from the Camorra. You promise me you will keep to the main road. Do not go off the beaten track – they would not dare to strike in full view of the public."

"You have received an actual threat from them?"

"I have heard they are furious with me for sealing the Benedetti deal. They might well try to prevent things from progressing. But, no need to worry unduly – follow my instructions and you will be safe. I have instructed the driver to arm himself, just in case."

Anthea tried not to show her alarm that matters had reached a point where it was necessary to have an armed escort when going out.

'I shall be sure that Linette knows the situation, just in case she is entertaining any foolish notions about giving me the slip,' she decided.

Later as the carriage pulled away, Anthea could not help but look for signs that they were being followed.

"You are rather jittery today," commented Linette. "You must not worry yourself unduly. I will not run away, you have my word."

"No, it is not that I disbelieve you – it's just that your father warned me again this morning that the Camorra are angry he has snatched the Benedetti contract away from Italian hands."

"Well, I am not going to let it stop me from having a really nice day. To think, Anthea! Roberto is going to paint me!"

"I thought he did not care for portraiture. That is what he told us the first day we met him."

"Oh, he says I inspire him and shown him the error of his ways. He cannot wait to portray me on canvas. I am hoping to give it to Papa when I marry Roberto."

"You are not still thinking of that nonsense? Your father does not deserve it – you know he dotes on you."

Linette scowled.

"I am twenty-one in two months and then we shall be free to marry, whether he gives us his blessing or not!"

"Linette, I am shocked at your attitude. Your father is a wonderful man who does not deny you a thing. How can you be so careless of his feelings?"

Linette paused and regarded Anthea closely.

"Why, I believe you are just a little bit in love with Papa!" she cried. "He often has that effect on ladies."

"You are mistaken," said Anthea, fussing with her umbrella to cover her confusion. "I just think that you are being a trifle impulsive."

"But Papa will soon wish to return to England now that his business is almost concluded – "

"Not so. He told me this morning we would stay in Naples for a while yet. So you see, there is no rush. Tell him about Roberto and let him become accustomed to the fact that you are together and in love and then he will come round to the idea."

Linette seemed placated by Anthea's suggestion.

She sank back and contented herself with watching people thronging through the bustling streets of Naples.

"It's going to rain today, which is a pity," remarked Linette, as their carriage neared Roberto's house. "Still it won't matter to Roberto as he is not painting the weather!"

Anthea chuckled.

"It is an honour to be an artist's muse and although Roberto is not so well-known at the moment, he will surely become one of the great names in art."

"I certainly believe so. Look, here we are. Are you coming inside, Anthea?"

"I will for a while and then I will ask the driver to take me sightseeing. Your father said that we should stick to the main roads for safety and there is a Church I wish to see that has an interesting archaeological history."

Linette appeared delighted that she was going to be left alone with Roberto.

She skipped lightly down the carriage steps to ring the doorbell, singing as she went.

Roberto opened the door and threw his arms around her.

"*Cara mia!*" he cried and then he spotted Anthea in the carriage.

"Signorina Preston, how nice to see you. Will you come in and have coffee and cakes?"

"Thank you. I hear you will be painting Linette."

"*Si*, in the garden. It will be beautiful, as she is!"

Anthea could not prevent herself from taking one last look over her shoulder as she entered Roberto's house.

Even though she was attempting to keep a brave face, she was really quite nervous.

Roberto was the perfect host, producing coffee and little Neapolitan pastries for them to savour.

"Although we have not long eaten breakfast, how could I refuse such a delight!" enthused Anthea, helping herself to what Roberto told her was called *sfogliatella*.

They chatted for a while and, seeing that Roberto was becoming anxious to start painting, she took her leave.

"I will return just after luncheon," she whispered to Linette. "Then we shall have to make our way back to the ship before the end of the afternoon."

Anthea climbed into the carriage and as they drove down the hill, she did not notice a ramshackle cart carrying a small group of rough-looking men pull out onto the road and start following them.

All through the congested streets they were keeping her carriage within sight.

After a bit, they drew closer to the Church Anthea was so keen to see. However the driver appeared perturbed about something.

He stopped the carriage and turned round to speak with her.

"I am so sorry, signorina," he apologised. "But *la strada*, it is too narrow for the carriage."

'Oh, I shall have to continue on foot,' she sighed, although, so far, the rain had held off, but she was certain that the clouds would burst at some point.

Climbing down from the carriage, she ordered the driver to wait for her in a side street.

"I will not be too long," she told him, as she tucked her umbrella under her arm. "Then I should like to go and find a nice café for luncheon if you can recommend one for me?"

The driver nodded and closed the carriage door.

Anthea scanned the hill in front of her.

Rows of white-washed houses rose up and the road seemed to become narrower as it reached the summit.

Using her umbrella as a walking stick she set off.

The road was very quiet as she started up the hill and she saw no one except a large black cat who sat washing itself on a balcony.

Recalling the Earl's warning, she wondered if she should return to the carriage, but then dismissed the idea.

'This is a very popular Church in Naples,' she told herself, 'and I cannot imagine there not being other people about. And although I cannot see anyone, we must have approached it via a different route to the one taken by most other tourists.'

As the driver pulled the carriage away into a side street, the men in the cart took his place.

Their cart was narrower and lighter than a carriage and they urged their horse up the hill closer behind Anthea.

'Goodness! It's a long way up,' she panted, as she paused to let a dog cart pass her.

The noise of his horse's hooves and the rattle of his wheels drowned out the sound of the cart in pursuit.

At last she reached the churchyard.

'Now where are these ancient ruins I have read so much about?' she wondered, scanning the tombs.

She moved off along the path and decided that there must be someone inside the Church who could point her in the right direction.

However, if she had turned she might have noticed two men creeping through the graves towards her, one of whom held a sack in his hands.

The entrance to the Church was at the back of the building and Anthea had to walk some distance to find it.

Just as she put her hand on the brass door to open it, she was grabbed from behind and, before she knew it, a sack was thrown over her body.

"Help! Help!" she cried out, dropping her umbrella. "*Aiuto!*"

But the men were too strong for her.

Almost as soon as the sack was over her head, they had fastened it with strands of heavy rope.

Her cries were so muffled they could not be heard.

Speaking to each other in a strange dialect she had not encountered before, the men dragged Anthea down the path to their waiting cart.

Inside the sack she was terrified.

Not only could she not see a thing, but she dreaded what might happen next.

'It must be the *Camorra*,' she thought, as the men roughly bundled her onto their cart.

Her elbows were grazed in the struggle and the thin cotton of her dress had ripped, exposing her delicate skin to the hairy material of the sack.

She winced with pain as the cart jolted into life.

'If I keep quiet then perhaps they will not harm me. I have often heard that it is best not to struggle if you do not wish to be hurt,' she tried to comfort herself.

'I hope the carriage driver realises that something is wrong and goes to raise the alarm.'

The journey was most unpleasant, jerking around in the cart with the top half of her body tied into the sack, she could neither see where she was going nor understand what the men were saying to each other.

'I had heard that there was a Neapolitan dialect, but I had not anticipated that it would be so hard to fathom,' she thought, as the cart came to a halt.

Before she knew it they had carried her kicking and screaming body from the cart into some building that was obviously their hideout.

Eventually, and after a long exchange of words, the sack was untied and, for the first time, she came face-to-face with her captors.

The three men were swarthy with rough faces and ill-fitting clothes.

They waved their arms as they spoke to each other and seemed to be disagreeing about something.

In the torrent of unfamiliar language, she caught the word 'Earl' and then 'daughter'.

'Goodness they think I am the Earl's daughter!' she felt shocked. 'It must be my colouring, although the Earl's hair is darker than mine, to an Italian we must look alike. With Linette having such different hair and eyes, it is no wonder they have made this mistake.'

She looked up at the tallest of the three and began to speak in Italian.

At once he paused and listened to her.

"Ah," he muttered menacingly. "You speak Italian. That makes it easier as we do not speak English, although Gianni here reads it quite well."

"Then, you must understand it when I tell you that you are mistaken. I am not who you think I am."

"You are the Earl of Hayworth's daughter."

"No, I am his daughter's chaperone."

The man laughed in her face.

"You think I am stupid? You are so like him! Look – same hair!"

He pulled roughly at an escaped curl and flicked it up in the air.

"No, you are wrong," she cried, trying to prevent the tears from flowing. "I tell you, I am not his daughter."

"You lie," snarled Gianni. "We have seen you go with him to his business meetings."

"But that is because I speak Italian and his daughter does not."

Gianni talked to the others and they cast suspicious looks in Anthea's direction.

After a long and furious debate the taller man came towards her.

"We are holding you to ransom and, unless the Earl backs out of the ship deal, we will kill you!"

"No! You cannot! He will not!" she yelled, almost fainting with horror and fear.

"Shut up!" shouted out Gianni, moving towards her with a threatening look on his face. "Now, you will write a letter to this English Earl and we will have it delivered. Do not try any tricks – I understand the English words even if I cannot speak them."

Gianni grabbed hold of her arm and dragged her to a small wooden table in the middle of the room.

Anthea's eyes had by now adjusted to the dim light and she saw that there was a sheet of paper laid on it.

"Here, write," he barked, then said something to his friends in Neapolitan.

As she took up the rough pencil he had given her to write the note, Anthea could not stop herself from crying.

Both her elbows were now sheer agony and she was feeling bruised and humiliated as well as utterly terrified.

Her hand shook as she tried to write with the thick pencil and her writing looked appallingly bad as a result.

As she wrote, she wracked her brains to think of a way to alert the Earl without Gianni noticing.

'I just cannot imagine that such an uncouth ruffian would be able to read English.'

"Why are you stopping?" he screamed, banging his fist on the table. "Write quickly! We want this delivered tonight. We will make plenty money out of you, *bella*!"

He pushed his face threateningly close to hers and pinched her cheek between his rough fingers. She shrank from his overpowering smell and went back to her task.

'I must not annoy him or he might kill me,' she told herself, finishing the note as best she could.

"Here," she said, handing it to Gianni. "Is this what you want?"

He took the note over to a window and pulled back the shutter just a fraction. He pored over the piece of paper and then nodded.

"Good," he growled. Then he folded it up carefully and gave it to the taller man.

'He must be the gang leader,' surmised Anthea, as she watched him leave the house and go out to the cart.

She now heard new voices outside and guessed that more men had arrived at the hideout.

'I hope they are not going to harm me anyway,' she thought, 'but surely the Earl will be coming to look for me soon? The driver must have realised something is wrong and has gone to sound the alarm. Oh, but he is dozy and what if he has fallen asleep?'

The leader of the gang came back and immediately ordered Gianni to take Anthea into another room.

He practically threw her inside it and then she heard the sound of a key in the lock.

Looking around, she saw that she was in a small bedroom with just a single bed and a chair in it. There was one tiny high window and everywhere was thick with dust.

'Not even a table and what if I want to wash?' she murmured, rubbing her sore elbows.

She sank down onto the bed and burst into tears.

'So what will become of me? Oh, Mama! Can you not do something to help me? Is there not some way you can make the Earl come and rescue me?'

She was still crying as Gianni came into the room with a glass of water –

*

As Anthea had suspected her lazy driver had indeed fallen asleep. He awoke after a long nap and, upon hearing the Church bells strike two o'clock, realised that something was dreadfully amiss.

"Signorina Preston!" he cried. "Signorina Preston."

He stumbled from the carriage and ran up the hill. Reaching the summit, he found the Church but no sign of Anthea.

"I must go back to the ship and alert his Lordship," he said, pushing through the crowds of tourists who stood around in the churchyard.

Jumping onto the carriage he whipped up the horses into action and drove off like fury.

"I must tell his Lordship! I am in such trouble!"

When he reached the ship, the Earl was up on deck enjoying a post-prandial stroll.

He had finished a delicious luncheon and thought he would like to enjoy the afternoon sun, when he saw the empty carriage rocketing through the crowds towards him.

'Something is very wrong here,' he said to himself, before shouting for Captain MacFarlane.

"My Lord!" cried out the hapless driver. "Signorina Preston – she has vanished!"

The Earl ran and shook him as hard as he could.

"And my daughter, where is she?"

"She is safe – we left her at the artist's house. But Signorina Preston – I took her to the Church on the hill and the road was too narrow – "

"You let her go on her own? You damned fool!"

For a moment Captain MacFarlane thought that the Earl would strike the cowering driver.

He stepped forward and touched him on the arm.

"My Lord, we should rush to that Church at once. Perhaps there is a plausible explanation for this. I know of that Church and the Priest is also known to me – perhaps he has seen Miss Preston."

The Earl let go of the driver with a sigh.

"You are right. The important thing is to find her without further ado. Could you muster a band of men and follow me in your carriage?"

"At once, my Lord."

Captain MacFarlane ran back up the gangplank.

The Earl, with a stern look at the cowering driver, ordered him to take him immediately to the Church.

"I want you to leave me at the exact spot where you dropped Miss Preston – and make haste, man,"

He jumped into the carriage and drew out the pistol that was kept underneath the seat.

'I may need this,' he murmured to himself checking it and then sliding it into his overcoat.

At the same time the Captain came charging down the gangplank with his group of men. They all leapt into a nearby carriage and Midshipman Jones took the reins.

"Let's go!" shouted the Earl.

The two carriages took off at speed in the direction of the Church. As they swept along, they almost knocked down a few pedestrians, such was their haste.

At last they reached the road where the driver had left Anthea.

"It was here, my Lord," he said, as he pulled the horses up short.

The Earl jumped down and waited for the Captain and his men to join him.

"Captain, you come with me. Midshipman Jones, you go with the driver to the house where my daughter was dropped off and fetch her back to the ship.

"*Now*," muttered the Earl under his breath, "we go and search for Miss Preston."

With grim expressions the small band advanced up the hill towards the Church. They soon made headway and came to a halt amongst the tombstones of the churchyard.

A group of tourists was just emerging from inside the Church and the Earl scanned the party hopefully.

But Anthea was not with them.

"Come, let's find this Priest," he insisted, indicating that they should all move forwards.

As they gathered at the Church door the Earl almost tripped over a long dusty object that lay in his path.

"What is this?" he cried, picking it up.

"It's a green umbrella, my Lord," answered Captain MacFarlane. "And I am certain that I saw Miss Preston with one just like that this morning when she left the ship with Lady Linette."

Bending down the Earl could quite clearly see the marks of a scuffle on the ground.

"*The Camorra*!" he breathed with an agonised look on his face.

Within seconds they were all running back to where Captain MacFarlane's men had left their carriage.

"Where are we headed?" asked the Captain. "It will not be easy to find the Camorra hideout, they are wily men who are highly adept at concealing their whereabouts."

"We are going to see Signor Benedetti. If anyone has an idea of where to find them, then he will. Come, we must hurry, there is no time to lose."

As they drove off, the Earl was thumping his fist repeatedly against his thigh, saying over and over again,

"Oh, God! If anything has happened to Anthea – I shall never forgive myself!"

CHAPTER TEN

Anthea watched miserably as the sun slowly sank in the sky plunging her into darkness inside her prison.

'I must be in a basement,' she now decided, as she shivered in the gloom, 'because I can hear people outside in the street and they seem to be floating above my head.'

She could hear sounds of heavy footsteps overhead and the sound of singing.

'Perhaps we are beneath a restaurant or tavern, but whereabouts we are in the City, I have no idea. I wish I could get my bearings.'

Her rumbling stomach reminded her that she had not eaten a thing since Roberto's delicious *sfogliatella*.

'Now I am glad I ate so much this morning, but I shall soon want something else. But do these men intend to starve me as well as hold me to ransom?'

Outside she could hear her captors' voices.

'They shout and I wish I could fathom their dialect and understand what they are arguing about. If it concerns me or the Earl, then I want to know.'

The three men were furiously berating the boy who had just arrived back, still holding the ransom note.

"The English Earl, he was not on the ship," pleaded the boy. "There was only a sentry and he would not let me past the gangplank."

"They must have found out that the girl is missing,"

said Gianni, "but how can we make our demands known if they do not know who has kidnapped her?"

"They will know," came in the tall man, with an air of assurance. "This Earl – he is not stupid – he will guess that we have taken action against him."

"But how will he find us?" bellowed the third man.

"We shall make his daughter write us another note and send it in the morning. They will never find us here, and by the time that the Earl has it, he will be so desperate to have her back, he will do whatever we ask."

"So, a delay could work in our favour. Excellent!" sneered Gianni.

The three men broke into hearty laughter, much to Anthea's consternation.

'What do they find so amusing?' she worried, her mind running riot. 'Have they yet decided what they will do with me? Surely the Earl will have their ransom note by now and will be on his way?'

But, as the hours ticked by and Gianni brought her a half-spent candle and a hunk from a stale loaf to eat, she began to lose hope.

*

Back at *The Sea Sprite*, a clearly distraught Linette had been brought back from Roberto's house and locked in her cabin on her father's orders.

Jackson greeted her grimly as she was escorted up the gangplank.

"I am sorry, my Lady, but these are his Lordship's orders. You are not to leave the ship until he returns."

"Is there any news at all of Anthea – I mean, Miss Preston?" she asked, as her bottom lip trembled.

"None, my Lady."

133

"Oh, it is all my fault!" she cried, rending her skirt with her hands. "If I had not been so selfish and intent on having my own way, Anthea would be safe."

Jackson steered a weeping Linette along the deck to the portside and then locked the cabin door behind her.

"You will come and inform me the moment there is any news, won't you?" she sobbed, as he turned the key.

*

The Earl and his party reached the Benedetti Office just as they were locking up.

"Signor Benedetti, where he is? It is most urgent that I see him," he demanded imperiously.

The clerk shook his head,

"*Mi dispiace, signor, non parlo inglese.*"

The Earl immediately understood what the man was saying. He repeated himself, this time in Italian.

"*É alla sua casa,*" said the man, writing an address.

The Earl took the piece of paper and showed it to Captain MacFarlane.

"Yes, I know this district well, my Lord. It's in the smarter part of the City."

"Come, we have no time to lose," insisted the Earl, leaping athletically into the carriage.

Sometime later he was knocking on the door of an immense villa surrounded by lush gardens and iron gates.

A servant answered the door and was stunned to see the grim-looking party standing in front of them.

"I must see Signor Benedetti at once!" ordered the Earl, stepping inside the hall.

The stunned servant stood with his mouth open, as the Earl repeated his request.

"It is all right, Cosmo," came a voice from the top of an imposing marble staircase. "I have been expecting this. My Lord Earl – it is the Camorra, *non*?"

"I am afraid so, they have kidnapped my daughter's chaperone."

"*La bellissima signorina* Preston," cried out Signor Benedetti. "This is terrible! What can I do to help? I have men of my own – "

"We need to find where they have taken her."

"Have they sent a ransom note yet? It is their usual way of doing things."

"I do not know – I left the ship the moment my man alerted me that she had gone missing."

"They will have sent one without doubt, demanding substantial sums of money and your withdrawal from our deal," sighed Signor Benedetti.

"Perhaps we should return to the ship?"

"No, they will be expecting you to do that. I know how desperate you are to find your Signorina Preston, but I advise caution. To outwit the Camorra, we have to be as crafty as they are."

"What do you suggest, Signor Benedetti?"

"Let me send for two sailors I know well. Although they work for me they move in the same circles as this lot."

"You hire criminals?" asked the Earl shocked.

"To be a step ahead of the Camorra, it is necessary for me to soil my hands," replied Signor Benedetti, ringing for his servant.

"Come, you and your men must rest awhile. I will send for my contacts. The Camorra will not do a thing until they have delivered the ransom note. Waiting for them is second nature."

Feeling rather uneasy, the Earl signalled to Captain MacFarlane and his crew to join him.

They sat down on the fine Venetian furniture in the drawing room and waited.

"It's getting dark," murmured Captain MacFarlane. "It will be harder to flush these men out at night."

"I have confidence in Signor Benedetti," replied the Earl. "He has no wish to be intimidated by these men and, furthermore, he knows that he will have to pay me a large amount of compensation if the deal does not go through – that is the Italian way."

The time ticked by and the Earl could not remain seated. He rose from his chair and began to pace the room.

'Anthea! I pray you are safe!' he said to himself, over and over again.

His patience was about to wear thin, when Signor Benedetti's doorbell rang.

Everyone leapt to their feet and moved towards the hall. Outside the sound of voices in the Neapolitan dialect could be heard conversing with Signor Benedetti.

"Do you follow what they are saying?" whispered the Captain.

"It's too dashed difficult," replied the Earl. "I have never mastered it and can make no sense of it at all."

At last Signor Benedetti came to join them with a smile on his face.

"Gentlemen, we are in luck," he started. "My men know exactly where to find them, they are outside and will take you to their hideout."

"Thank you, *thank you* so much," replied the Earl, shaking his hand warmly.

"I am afraid I cannot come with you, but I will be

waiting for news. Promise me you will send word when you have liberated Signorina Preston?"

"I will."

The Earl ran outside to where the two sailors were waiting and although they did not understand English, the Earl managed to converse with them in Italian.

Soon, they were all on their way – into the depths of Naples where no foreigner would dare set foot.

The further they advanced into the docks area, the more the Captain's men seemed uneasy.

"Captain," cautioned Midshipman Jones, "this is no place for a gentleman like his Lordship."

"His Lordship is more than capable of taking care of himself," retorted the Captain.

But even he began to feel nervous as the two sailors produced pistols and asked Midshipman Jones in Italian to halt the carriage.

Pulling up the horses, the crew watched as the two sailors jumped out. They crept into a nearby tavern and a few moments later emerged shaking their heads.

"They are not there?" asked the Earl.

"*Non*," replied the sailors.

They made another stop and the Captain noticed the Earl becoming increasingly agitated.

"There is still hope, my Lord. Remain steadfast."

"You are right," replied the Earl. "But it is now so dark and I fear for her. It is not safe for even us to be out in this place, let alone a young woman."

"They will almost certainly have her hidden away and she will not be out wandering the streets."

The carriage halted once again and the two sailors climbed out and entered another even seedier tavern.

But this time when they emerged, they had satisfied looks on their faces.

"It is here," they indicated quietly. "The hideout is in a basement beneath this tavern."

"Right, men. This is what we do," ordered the Earl, taking charge. "I will investigate the area with one of you, while the others stay on lookout. Signor Benedetti's sailors – you go into the tavern and look out in case they try and escape out the back way."

"Aye-aye, my Lord," they all chorused.

The Earl then drew out his pistol from his coat and, taking Midshipman Jones, he crept along the outside wall of the tavern, searching frantically for an entrance.

"My Lord – look. There's a window there, it might be something?"

He followed Midshipman Jones's finger and could just make out a dirty window at the foot of the tavern wall.

Looking over his shoulder the Earl crept over to the window.

Bending down, he tried to get a good look, but the panes were too filthy for him to see through.

Taking out his lawn handkerchief, he rubbed at the glass and removed just enough dirt so that he could view what lay inside.

What he saw made his heart leap, for there, sitting hunched over a lone candle and weeping, was *Anthea*!

He tore off his overcoat and picked up a rock lying nearby. Wrapping the rock in his coat he smashed through the filthy window – much to Anthea's shock.

"Anthea," he hissed through the broken glass.

"My Lord!" she cried out, turning her white face to him. "*You have come*! I prayed and prayed you would."

"Now don't make a noise. Here is what we will do. I have my men with me and we are all armed."

Anthea looked alarmed.

"Don't worry – you will be safe if you do exactly as I tell you," he whispered. "Stay quiet and then hide under the bed as soon as you hear us break down their entrance door, is that clear?"

"Do be very careful, my Lord?" she beseeched him, stretching her hand up to the broken window to touch his.

The Earl took her cold hand carefully and squeezed her fingers.

"I will. Climb down and be ready to get under the bed. Remember – as soon as you hear us break in, you must hide yourself."

Anthea gazed into those warm amber eyes and her heart went out to him.

'*How I love him*! I cannot pretend otherwise,' she sighed, as she crouched by the bed.

Silently the Earl motioned to Midshipman Jones to follow him and they started to run round the building.

Halfway they met the Captain who was standing by a concealed entrance that led down to a basement.

"It is here," whispered the Captain.

"Everybody ready?" hissed the Earl quietly.

The four men nodded in unison.

"On the count of four, we break down the door – one, two, three, *four*!"

With a frantic leap the Earl threw himself headlong at the door shoulder-first and the door cracked open.

"Good work, my Lord!" cried the Captain, as they all ran inside, firing their pistols at the ceiling.

At the first shot Anthea dived under the bed and lay there quaking. She could hear shouting and the sounds of fighting – and then more shots – and then it all went quiet.

Her heart was beating so fast, it made her feel ill.

There was no sound coming from the other room and, as she crouched beneath the bed in the dirt and dust, she convinced herself that the Earl had been shot and that, any moment, the Camorra men would burst into the room and kill her too.

She closed her eyes and started to pray fervently – to her Mama in Heaven and to God.

'Please keep the Earl safe,' she pleaded desperately, more concerned for his well-being than for her own.

She was still lying in the dirt with her hands tightly clasped together when the door to the room burst open.

She screwed up her eyes and was moving her lips in prayer as footsteps drew near.

"Anthea, it's safe for you to come out now – my darling, are you all right?"

Filled with joy, she crawled out from under the bed and leapt straight into the Earl's arms.

"Darling Anthea!" he cried, stroking her bedraggled hair and dirty face. "I was so dreadfully worried."

Then, his lips moved towards hers as he pulled her closer.

Anthea could scarcely believe what was happening as she sank into a passionate kiss that went on forever.

Pulling back from him, she fluttered her eyelids – feeling certain that she would swoon.

"Am I dreaming?" she murmured, her mouth still quivering from his kiss.

"No, my darling one. This is real. I was so worried

about you. I have only just realised what you mean to me and I would have died had anything happened to you."

"Can this really be true?" she stammered, taking his handsome face in her hands.

His amber eyes were like deep dark pools of love as he looked down at her.

"It is true," he answered, kissing her eyes and then her forehead. "I love you and never want to be away from your side."

Just then the Captain came into the room.

"My Lord, the Police are outside. Someone must have called them. They wish to speak with you and to see if Miss Preston is safe and well."

"She could not be safer," he replied holding Anthea close and gazing into her eyes. "My darling one, I must go and speak with them. Captain MacFarlane will assist you. There is a carriage outside waiting to take you back to *The Sea Sprite*."

In the street the Policemen had all three Camorra in handcuffs about to take them away.

As Anthea was helped into a carriage, Gianni threw her a look of hatred.

"You are dead!" he spat at her in English.

"Do not pay any heed to him," said the Captain as he settled her down. "He is a doomed man and will be thrown into prison for many years. It is rare for the Police to intervene in Naples with the Camorra, but as the Earl is involved and they want to avoid an international incident, they really have no choice."

"Who called them?"

"It may have been Signor Benedetti himself, but it might have been a local. We made so much noise breaking into the basement that they probably heard us on Capri!"

141

Anthea laughed weakly.

She was so exhausted that all she wanted to do was sleep in the Earl's arms.

Yet she felt unbelievably exhilarated.

'He loves me! He loves me!' she told herself with a secret smile. 'I cannot believe it, but it's true.'

The Earl finished talking to the Police and watched as they started off with the three Camorra ruffians in the back of their wagon.

He then asked the Captain to go and find Signor Benedetti's two sailors in order to thank them.

"Make certain that they are well rewarded," he said, pulling out a sheaf of high-denomination lira notes.

The Captain saluted and the Earl ran to the carriage, and climbed in beside Anthea.

Putting his arm around her, he ordered Midshipman Jones, who sat on the box, to take them back to the ship as quickly as possible.

"Has Linette returned?" Anthea asked him, as the carriage pulled off down the street.

"I had her brought back to *The Sea Sprite*," replied the Earl. "She is safe and well."

He did not mention Roberto and nor did Anthea.

Rather, she let herself sink wordlessly against him, enjoying the feeling of his warmth against her aching skin.

*

Back at *The Sea Sprite*, everywhere was alive with the sound of running feet and men shouting as the carriage containing the Earl, Anthea and their fellow crew members drew up alongside on the quay.

"They have returned!" went up the shout.

The Earl and the Captain helped Anthea aboard as Midshipman Jones brought up the rear with the rest of the crew.

Everyone saluted as they came on board.

"Send for the ship's doctor," called the Captain, as the Earl carried Anthea into the Saloon.

"Is Lady Linette in her cabin?" asked the Earl, as he placed Anthea gently down on a sofa.

"Yes, my Lord," replied one of the crew.

"Will you go to her and let her know that we are all safe and unharmed?"

"At once, my Lord!"

Jackson appeared with water and a bottle of brandy.

"Anthea, would you mind if I left you for a while?" murmured the Earl tenderly as he stroked her hair and gave her a glass of water.

"Linette?"

"Yes. I have been far too indulgent with her and it is time for me to remind her of her duties as my daughter. Perhaps I have only myself to blame."

"You are too hard on yourself. Linette is a wilful young lady, as I have discovered."

The Earl discreetly squeezed her hand and then left the cabin.

Then the ship's doctor arrived to examine Anthea. He pronounced her well if a little shaken and prescribed lots of rest.

He was just departing when the Earl reappeared.

"Is she all right?" he asked anxiously.

"She will be fit as a fiddle, my Lord, once she has rested. It has been a terrible shock to her, but she will soon recover," responded the doctor.

With that the Earl then shooed everyone out of the Saloon and locked the door behind them.

"Sh! Don't worry, I want us to be undisturbed," he insisted, smiling at Anthea's alarmed look.

Rushing over to the sofa he took Anthea in his arms and, before she knew it, he was kissing her once again.

Her spirit soared up to Heaven as she gave herself up to his insistent lips.

As they parted, the Earl gazed into her eyes with so much love that she wondered if she was dreaming.

"I thought I had lost you before I had even told you how much I love you," he breathed.

"Then my heart rejoices to be safe here with you. For I love you too. I have thought of nothing but you since I met you in England."

"Since England? But you gave me no sign that you had feelings for me."

"How could I when, to all intents and purposes, you were my employer? You did not know who I was or even where I came from and so I naturally assumed you would never consider me."

"I would not care a jot if you were the daughter of a cowherd!" cried the Earl, holding her hand and stroking it. "I would still have fallen in love with you. And to think – I had given up all hope of ever finding love – "

Anthea stopped for a moment.

'What is he saying?' she thought, not understanding his meaning.

"But surely, you had given up hope of ever finding love *again*," she questioned him after a moment.

The Earl looked at her and then sighed.

"The truth is, Anthea, that I have never been in love before. I did not love my wife –

"There have been women since Maureen died, but none who could hold a candle to you and none I loved."

"But your wife – you are really saying you did not love her? Then why did you marry her?"

"It is a great secret and one that even Linette does not know," sighed the Earl. "And I hope you will not think ill of me after hearing it. Do you love me enough for me to tell you what even Linette has no knowledge of?"

Anthea's stomach began to churn as her heartbeat quickened.

She felt slightly sick with anticipation.

'What could it be that he is about to tell me?' she wondered frantically before saying,

"Please continue, my Lord."

He took a deep breath and held her hand tighter.

"It is a long story. Even though I am now the Earl, I was the younger brother. I had an older brother, Fulton, who married to please our father. It was not a love match, but a good one, uniting two of the most powerful families in Surrey.

"But then one day the family business took him to Scotland to oversee the building of a ship in Glasgow."

"And there?"

"And there he fell in love with Maureen a local girl. You will forgive me for being forthright, but it is necessary for you to know all the unpalatable facts. She became with child and the scandal threatened to ruin the family name.

"The shock of it all killed our father and he dropped dead a few months before Maureen was due to give birth.

"Maureen's father was understandably furious and demanded that my brother should marry his daughter. But, as Fulton was already married, he obviously could not and divorce would have created an even worse scandal."

"I don't understand where you fit into this story."

"I offered to marry Maureen in order to save further scandal. I was almost sixteen and if my brother could not rescue the family honour, then I felt compelled to act like a man and save the day."

"And the child – is Linette?" stammered Anthea, as the truth slowly dawned upon her.

"Yes. With Fulton now the Earl, he gave me lands and a house in Scotland that belonged to our family, so that Maureen, the child and I could then settle down, bringing up Linette as my own."

"Such an amazing noble deed!" exclaimed Anthea. "But I sense there is more?"

"Yes, indeed. Unfortunately double tragedy struck. My brother went to India with a new ship and the Russians sank it off the coast of Gujarat and he was never found.

"As I was now the Earl, it was decided that it would be best if my family and myself moved down to London. By this time, Maureen was carrying our own child, but the journey South was long and difficult.

"As soon as we arrived in Park Lane she miscarried and died of complications. I saw no point in telling Linette about her real parentage, so continued the deception to this day."

"So Linette is not your daughter! And she does not know this?"

"No, I have brought her up as my own."

"This explains so much," sighed Anthea, getting up from the sofa and walking towards the porthole. "I could not understand how one so young had a grown-up daughter and also, how you did not really resemble each other."

"That is because she is the image of her mother. It is no wonder that the gang thought you were my daughter as your colouring is quite similar to mine."

"Yes, that is what I believed too," she said, sinking down on a nearby chair.

Anthea could scarcely take it all in – there was so much she had not known.

And Linette?

She could not imagine how she would feel if she discovered that she herself was the result of an adulterous relationship. It was both shocking and scandalous.

The Earl then moved towards Anthea and looked gravely down at her.

"Please say you will still love me now that I have told you everything? Please don't refuse to have me!"

"Elliot, it has only made me love you more," cried Anthea, turning her face up towards him. "I too confess to harbouring a secret, although it is not about me, it is about Linette."

"I already know all about this Roberto," interrupted the Earl. "Never mind what Linette says, do *you* believe that she loves him and wants to marry him?"

Yes," answered Anthea in a low voice. "And what is more she is so completely determined that she plans to marry him in secret so that she does not have to return to England."

"She had alluded as much," countered the Earl. "I think I had better meet Roberto as soon as possible. After what has happened to you, I feel we should leave Naples before long, but not before we have married!"

Anthea leapt up and threw her arms round his neck, kissing him over and over again.

"Would you, Anthea? *Would you marry me*?"

"I will! Oh, I will!" she cried, kissing him again. "I had thought that after Jolyon, I would never feel like this or love again. Shall we go and tell Linette now?"

"No, wait – I want to stay in your arms just a little longer," murmured the Earl, as he kissed her.

Pulling away, he smiled at her,

"It must have been a very lucky star that brought us together. Fate has, indeed, worked in a mysterious way for you *are* that lucky star!"

"I would love to think so or maybe it was Mama in Heaven smiling on us. Two lonely people searching – who found each other – and love.

"Now come along, I think I heard Roberto outside on deck – let us not delay – the quicker you meet him and approve of him, the sooner we can get married – perhaps, a *double* wedding is in order?"

Anthea then entwined her arm through his and they unlocked the Saloon door and emerged out into the evening air much to the amazement of the assembled crew who had been waiting outside for news.

"Look, the moon is rising and the stars, have you ever seen anything more brilliant?" whispered the Earl, as they moved along the gangway to where Linette stood with Roberto.

As soon as she saw them coming towards her, she pulled away from Roberto, a guilty expression on her face.

"Anthea," she began. "I am so very sorry."

"Hush! Linette. Your father and I have something important to tell you."

Linette stared at her father and then at Anthea, who stood before her, so obviously together.

"You – and Papa?" she stammered. "I just do *not* believe it."

"I have asked Anthea to be my wife and *she has accepted*," confessed the Earl.